MICHELLE LYNN ROSS

Literally In Love

FAWN
CREEK
PRESS

*For Mrs. Meek, Mrs. Draper, Mrs. Faulkenberry, and Mr. Ellis—
My English teachers, thank you for making me who I am.*

Contents

Acknowledgments

What an amazing feeling to have another book to share with all of you! And none of this would be possible without my support system.

First and foremost, a huge thank you to my husband. Not only does he support all of my dreams, no matter how crazy they may seem, but he's also the best unpaid employee who is always up for driving me to events, carrying heavy boxes full of books, and buying me lunch afterward. Thank you for everything you do for me.

Thank you to my kids for being my biggest cheerleaders. I love you.

Thank you to my mom for always being willing to help when I'm busy doing bookish things. My household would be lost without you!

A million thanks to my proofreading team. These books shine because of you ladies, and your willingness to help me time and time again means the world to me!

To my writing friends—thank you for being my sounding board and for pushing me outside my comfort zone. You are the ones who make this job fun, and I couldn't have chosen better co-workers.

Thank you to the indie bookstores that have taken a chance on me and shelved my books. Your belief in me still blows me away.

And lastly, thank you to my readers. Thank you for reading my books, sharing my books, and taking the time to come see me at events. Your encouragement is what keeps me going. I hope to share stories with you for years to come.

Chapter 1

"Mom, seriously. I'm fine. Just because I'm thirty and single doesn't mean I'm going to die alone." I stand with my back to her as I load the last of the remaining closing dishes into the dishwasher. I press start and turn to face her, crossing my arms in front of my chest. "You don't have to worry about me."

My mother frowns, the worry lines on her forehead, the ones I'm sure I caused her to have, deepen as she slides onto a stool in the back corner of the kitchen. We are in the diner that my parents own, and I've just helped cover a shift for them.

Her voice softens. "I just worry about you. I worry that you don't put yourself out there enough or maybe that you've given up on love altogether. I want you to know that a happy life is possible. You *might* have to work for it a little harder than other people... and probably lower your standards a little."

Carefully, I step closer to my mother, keeping my voice soft and steady. "Sorry, the dishwasher is so loud that I think I misheard you. I could have sworn you just told me that I need to lower my standards."

She tightens her lips. "No, you heard me correctly."

"So, you're saying that I need to settle? Really? You know I'm only thirty, right?"

Mom lets out a heavy sigh. "No. That's not what I'm saying.

I'm just suggesting that maybe you need to put yourself out there. Take a chance with someone that you might not usually go on a date with. Or maybe put yourself on one of those dating apps on your phone. What's the one I'm thinking of? Tinder?"

I blink slowly. Partially curious about where my sixty-year-old mother might have learned of Tinder, but also completely flabbergasted that she just suggested I download a hookup app. I open my mouth to respond, but I'm interrupted by my father walking through the swinging kitchen door.

"Alright, ladies. The last customers of the night are gone, and we are closed. How's it going back here?" He unties his worn black apron and removes it from around the back of his neck. Then, he hangs it on the hook next to the door, just like he's done for the last thirty-five years.

I smirk. "Well, Mom was just suggesting that I find myself a booty call."

Mom scoffs and gently smacks me with the dishtowel in her hand. "That is not what I said. I simply suggested that she get on a dating app."

I turn towards my father. "She suggested that I use Tinder, which is pretty famously known to be used for hookups. I'd keep an eye on her if I were you."

"I didn't know that's what Tinder was for. I just knew the name." Mom groans, standing from her seat and moving towards my father. "I just don't want you to give up on finding your happily ever after. True love is real. Just look at your father and me."

My father wraps an arm around my mother's waist before leaning down to kiss the top of her head as if to prove her point further.

I shake my head and dig my hand into my apron pocket to

pull out my tip money from my evening. "You know, when I agreed to come help cover the closing shift, I didn't know that I was going to be getting a lecture as well."

Dad chuckles. "That was just a bonus lesson. Besides, don't act like you don't enjoy waiting tables. You're so good at it, and the customers love you."

"That's because I've been waiting on the same customers since I was fifteen and you could legally put me to work." I tease. "But, yes. I do enjoy it and truly don't mind helping out here and there."

"It reminds me of the good old days," Dad adds with a nostalgic grin.

"And to think. If I had a husband and a bunch of kids at home, you guys would have to find someone else to come cover your shifts."

"We would manage," Mom assures me.

"You always have," I agree. "Well, if we are done here, I'm going to get home. I have some work to finish before Christmas break is over."

"Absolutely. Thanks for your help tonight, kiddo." Dad says, following me through the kitchen so he can lock the door behind me, as always. He and Mom will stay for at least another hour to count money and prepare for tomorrow. Luckily, they live in the apartment upstairs, so their journey won't be long, and I don't have to worry about them getting home.

I rotate the lock on the glass door and turn to look at my father. "Night, Dad. Love you."

He smiles softly, and the wrinkles around his tired eyes have grown more prominent than I've noticed in a while. "Love you, too, Kris. And don't let your mom get to you too much. She wants to see you happy."

"I know," I whisper. "And I know happily ever after is real. It just hasn't been my turn to find it yet." I assure him.

"Your time is coming. I know it."

"That sounds like a threat." I deadpan.

He lets out a throaty chuckle. "It's a promise. Night, Kristen."

We say our good-byes, and I step out the door, making a mad dash for my car. My black Altima is older than I'd like to admit, but it still runs, so there's no point in upgrading it. I crank the heater to combat the chill of the Kansas winter, but it's no use. The air blowing from the vents is just barely warm by the time I drive the three blocks to my house.

I kill the engine and pause, looking up at my cute little home. It's dark outside, and the only light coming from the house is the soft glow of my Christmas tree shining through the front window.

I didn't do much to decorate for Christmas this year. There was no point. I don't do a lot of entertaining, so no one was here to see it other than me. I didn't even take my ornaments down from the attic. So I just put up my artificial pre-lit tree and left it alone.

Per usual, we visited my brother, Greg, and his family in Houston over the holidays. Greg and his wife, Mikayla, both work for a major oil company. Just a few years ago, they were transferred to the Texas branch. With three small kids and busy jobs, it only makes sense for us to travel to see them. My parents even close down the diner for a few days every Christmas and Thanksgiving so that they can enjoy the trip.

Since coming home, I've been meaning to take down the tree and tuck it away in the garage for next year, but I just can't.

Something about the soft glow of the white bulbs, the only

light in the living room, soothes me. I love sitting in silence next to the tree in the morning, sipping my coffee, and getting ready to start my day. Surprisingly, my cats have left it alone, so I'm in no hurry. Maybe I'll never take it down. Not that anyone would notice, I rarely have visitors anyway.

I run a bath and settle into the steaming hot water, relaxing for the first time since I rolled out of bed this morning. Leaning my head against my inflatable bath pillow, I close my eyes and try to rest for just a bit, but naturally, that doesn't last for long.

Jinx, my newest cat, a fuzzy little black guy with deep amber eyes, jumps up and lands on the edge of the tub. He meows loudly, commanding my attention, as he often does.

I pet the side of his head with my one dry hand, causing a purr to rise from his throat. "I'm sorry, buddy. I know you don't like being home alone, but I had to work today."

He meows again, softer this time, as though he's telling me that he accepts my apology. Then, he hops down from his perch. He circles once and lies on the black, fuzzy bathmat next to the tub.

Ever since I got this guy, a rescue from the local shelter, he has been by my side every second I am home. While I'm gone, he loves to patrol the neighborhood, but as soon as I come home, he can't get enough of me. I think we might be kindred spirits.

Maybe my mom is on to something about her concern about me being alone. I'm sure from her standpoint, I appear to be quite pitiful. When I'm not teaching high school English to a bunch of kids who have no interest in learning about grammar and punctuation, I'm picking up shifts at my parents' diner, or I'm sitting at home carrying on a full conversation with one of my three cats.

After scrubbing the scent of French fries and grilled onions from my hair and body, I dry off and change into the new lounge set my sister-in-law gifted me for Christmas. It's a soft waffle blend set, in dark green, one of my favorite colors. Then, I make a cup of tea and walk across the house to my spare bedroom.

Using the key that I pulled from my nightstand, I unlock the door and step inside the room. I don't turn on the overhead lights; instead, I switch on the table lamp next to my computer, and a soft glow fills the room. It's just enough to illuminate the pastel pink walls and the shelves of books lining the walls.

I settle into my white leather chair and cover myself with a floral throw blanket before Jinx hops into my lap, assuming his regular position.

While I wait for my computer to come to life, I complete the final task in my nightly routine, lighting a vanilla-scented candle. Something about the smell causes me to feel more creative than any other scent. I can't explain it. This is just the routine that works for me.

Using my keyboard, designed to look and sound like a typewriter's keys, I enter the password to unlock my computer and get to work. But I don't reach for lesson plans or papers that need grading. Those tasks were handled long before Christmas break ever began.

Instead, I focus on my second job. The job that gives me the creative outlet that I crave, but that no one in my life knows about. And if I have it my way, they never will.

Chapter 2

I pull into a parking spot at Fawn Creek High School and pause to look up at the building in front of me.

We've been out of school since the week before Christmas, and I've stayed away from school duties as much as possible during our break.

Looking back, it's funny to see how much I've changed over the years. When I first started teaching, my breaks were used for grading, lesson planning, and working on my classroom.

If I wasn't working in the building, I was working at home. If I wasn't doing either of those things, I was helping my parents with their restaurant. I was always busy, but somehow, nothing I was busy doing was actually for me. I was sad, tired, and burnt out.

That is, until the day everything changed.

I always loved to write when I was younger. I was the kid with the notebooks full of short stories piled high on my bedside table. There was always some story running through my head, and the only way to get it out was to write it down. So, I did.

As a teen, my personality changed, but my writing style never did. My favorite color was black, and every rock band T-shirt in my closet made that very clear. My general wardrobe was a Korn or Limp Bizkit baby-doll shirt, wide-leg Junco jeans, and my black Doc Martin combat boots. I thought I was so cool.

My dad always made fun of my pants, and looking back now, I was asking for it. I could, and sometimes did, fit an entire two-liter bottle of soda in the back pocket of those jeans.

But, despite the teasing, I loved my style. It made me feel edgy and mysterious. Even though I was going home and sitting down to write stories of relatable characters finding love against all odds, and finding a happily ever after.

Don't get me wrong, I tried to write in a way to match the way I looked, but I could never pull it off.

Every time I tried to write a thriller or something mysterious, it was garbage. It wasn't where my heart was, and that was clear in my writing. I never could get my insides to match my outward appearance, no matter how hard I tried.

Over the years, life got busy, and my writing time got less and less. Instead of writing for fun, I was writing essays for college or working to try to keep myself out of debt while I was in school to become a teacher.

It had been years since I last picked up a pen to write anything other than a lesson plan. That is, until one fateful winter evening, just about five years ago.

I was having one of my typical weekday evenings. Dinner was over, the house was clean, and I was cuddled alone on the sofa with my cat, a black and gray kitten named Ash.

I had just finished watching some silly little Christmas movie on TV. It was nothing special. I couldn't even tell you the name of it now, but they're all the same, aren't they?

A girl comes to a small town during the holidays. She accidentally runs into the town handyman/baker/lawyer/whatever. They end up as enemies until they are forced to work together to save Christmas. Shockingly, they fall in love and wind up living happily ever after in that tiny town.

The movie ended. The credits rolled, and I had a thought.

If other people can write these stories, why can't I?

So I did.

That night, I got to work on writing the first draft of my first novel.

It was terrible, as all first drafts are, but by the time I went back to school from Christmas break, I had a completed first draft.

I worked on it over the rest of the winter, changing things here and there, learning about dialogue, three-part structure, and everything else I could in the world of romance writing. I even hired an editor from Australia to see if I had anything worth printing.

She emailed me back with a manuscript covered in red ink and an encouraging note.

You have a gift for this. Keep going. The world needs the stories you are writing. We all need some happily ever after.

So, I kept going. I made the changes she suggested and worked hard all spring and summer to make my books shine.

I designed a cover, and by the time summer break was ending, my first book was ready to be published.

I opted to use a pen name because I had no intention to take this seriously. I figured I would self-publish the novel, and if it sucked, then no one in my life would ever know that I wrote a crappy little love story. No harm. No foul.

Besides, I'm a high school English teacher in a small town. The idea of my students somehow getting their hands on my book was enough to solidify my decision to stay discreet.

So, just like that, Maisie Bloomfield was born.

By the time that first book was published, I was already deep into writing book two—another small-town romance set in a fictional Kansas town. Another story that no one knew I had written.

Fast forward five years, and I've fallen into a steady rhythm. I'm publishing an average of three books a year.

It's slower than some, but faster than others. The fact that I'm single and child-free helps allow me to be so productive, especially during breaks from school.

This year, over Christmas break, I reached a milestone. I published my fifteenth book, and still, no one in my life has a clue.

But, instead of celebrating that accomplishment, I'm keeping it a secret as I head into work. I'll spend the day standing under fluorescent lights while I teach English to a bunch of teenagers who would rather be anywhere but here.

I climb out of my car and wrap my down-filled coat close to my body as I make my way towards the school.

It's still early, so there are no students on campus quite yet, allowing me to really take in the building that's been a part of my life since I was thirteen years old.

Though the property is quite old, the district does a great job at upkeep for the sake of the community. The building is really nothing more than a giant rectangle with a small cutout on one side for a courtyard. A courtyard where I will take my kids outside in the Spring so we can sit in the shade and enjoy some fresh air while they read.

The front of the building is plain but clean with a brick exterior. There is a large lawn filled with small trees, a tall flagpole, and a bronze statue of our school mascot, The Fawn

Creek Prairie Dog.

In front of the building is a large circular drive where parents can drive up to drop off their kids. It seems like just yesterday my mom was driving through that lane to drop me off for junior high.

High school was not the best time of my life, but there is still no place in the world that I would rather teach. I love my hometown, and I love the kids that I get to spend my days with, even when they roll their eyes at me for correcting their grammar.

I badge my way into the building and unlock my classroom door. My hand pauses at the light switch, but I only turn on one set of fluorescent bulbs. Once the area in front of the blackboard is illuminated, I get to work turning on my collection of table lamps and white Christmas lights strung throughout the room.

The kids think that I am doing them a favor by not forcing them to sit in a bright classroom first thing in the morning, but in reality, this is for me. The combination of the dim lights mixed with the pot of coffee I'll be drinking for the majority of the morning is exactly what I need to make it through the day—especially the first day back after Christmas break.

I start my coffee pot and unpack my teacher bag for the day. By the time I'm settled, it's nearly eight o'clock, and it's time for class to start.

The first hour passes quickly, with nothing notable happening. However, the second hour is a different story.

I'm sitting at my desk when my second hour students start trickling in. It's a mixture of seniors who definitely look like they are ready to finish off their last semester of high school and a handful of juniors who look like they crawled out of bed three seconds earlier. Everything about the scene is typical for a Monday morning.

Until it's not.

Becca, one of my juniors, slides into her seat and starts digging through her bag. She piles her typical class supplies on her desk: a notebook, a textbook, and her Chromebook. But the last thing that comes out of her leopard print backpack causes me to look twice. Not that I need to, I would recognize that cover anywhere.

The cover of Maisie Bloomfield's first book.

My mouth goes dry, and my pulse quickens.

One of my students is reading my book in my classroom. And she has no idea that I'm Maisie.

Now, I'm not worried about the content. My books are closed-door, so nothing explicit happens on the page. There's some swearing, but nothing worse than what I hear from these kids in the halls when they think I'm not listening.

No, it's more than that. I've worked for years to build my own reputation here, and it's working for me. The kids know that when they see me, Kristen Calhoun, I'm an authority figure. I'm not their friend. I'm not here to gossip or let them get away with crap. I'm here to ensure they work hard, learn the material, and graduate high school with a basic understanding of grammar and literacy. I have worked hard to protect my private life, or lack thereof, from them. As far as they know, I don't have a life outside of this classroom, besides waiting tables for my parents.

And somehow it's worked. They respect me, and they kid around with me, without taking it too far. If they know I write cute little lighthearted rom-coms, they are going to know I'm a fraud. They are going to know that deep down, I'm a softie who loves flowers and romance and the color pink.

They are going to see the personality that I have worked so hard to hide all these years.

I'm still working to formulate my thoughts regarding Becca's book when another student speaks.

"Oh, good. You got it!" Sadie, another junior, chimes in. "I got the second one. So, when you finish, we can trade." Sadie slides the book from her bag, holding up the second book in Maisie's series. "I have books 3 through 5 on the way."

I blink slowly. *What is happening?*

"Have you ever heard of Maisie Bloomfield, Ms. Calhoun?" Sadie asks.

"No..." I stutter. "I sure haven't."

Becca waves me off. "You probably wouldn't like her."

I raise a brow. Now, I'm intrigued. "Why's that?"

Sadie shrugs. "Well, I just don't think she writes your type of books. She writes rom-coms."

"What do you think I read?"

"I just assume you read non-fiction strictly. Self-Help, True Crime, that kind of thing." Becca admits. "Her books are sweet and funny and just feel like a warm hug in the middle of a town square. Not your type."

I snicker, relieved. "So, I'm that easy to read, huh?"

"Afraid so," Sadie shrugs. "Anyway, Maisie's books are popping off on TikTok right now. So, our book club has decided to read them all. There are fifteen total. I bought the first one this weekend, and we are each buying four more. We will trade them back and forth until we've read them all."

My eyes widen. "That's... a lot of money on books."

I have to admit the thought of my students dropping that kind of money on my books makes me feel uneasy.

"Worth it," Sadie tells me as the bell rings overhead, alerting us to the start of class. "Anyway, I'm surprised you haven't seen her on your TikTok."

I shake my head. "I don't really do any social media."

And, I mean it. I have a Facebook account that I rarely log in to, but none of the rest of that stuff.

And Maisie? She has no internet presence. She has no reason for one.

So, how is she all over TikTok? I make a mental note to find out tonight, even if it means downloading the app myself. But, in the meantime, I have a class to teach.

"Alright, ladies and gentlemen, get your journals out. I want you to stretch your muscles and get used to being back in the building. Today's writing prompt is, *What I did over Christmas Break.*

I hate to admit it, but the students' groans as they get out their supplies are music to my ears.

When I started teaching, I told the kids that the first thing I was bringing back was the journaling they used to do every morning in Kindergarten.

Most of them thought I was crazy, but their parents think I'm a genius. It's a great way to get their minds going in the morning, and today it's especially helpful.

It's the perfect way to keep them busy while I figure out how to deal with my students reading my books.

I sit down at my desk and sip my coffee, thinking over my conversation with the girls while I stare at my book sitting on Becca's desk.

I have to admit, seeing my book in the wild tugs at my heartstrings just a bit. Of course, I've seen the books in person.

I have my own copies. I order a copy of each book after it's published and tuck it away on a shelf in my office. But to see one in real life, in the hands of someone else? It's mind–blowing. And a little scary. I feel like I'm walking on the edge of being found out.

But the girls said it themselves. Maisie's books aren't my type. They are happy, pink, and flowery. They are nothing at all like the Ms. Calhoun they know. And that is enough reassurance that they will never find out my secret.

I have nothing to worry about.

Chapter 3

By lunchtime, my day has returned to semi-normal. The kids have come to class, done their work, and I've heard no other mention of Maisie Bloomfield. Thank goodness.

I've almost forgotten that the girls in second period are reading my silly little love stories until I walk into the cafeteria.

It's not just the girls from the school book club.

With a quick scan around the room, I estimate that there must be at least ten copies of my books in this cafeteria right now. Some are open and being read, some are stacked on top of textbooks... and I even see one poking out of the unzipped top of a backpack.

I'm not a Math teacher, but ten books out of the seventy kids in the room are not odds that are working for me. And only about half of the high school student body is in this lunch period.

This can not be happening.

"Hey, Ms. Calhoun," Willow, a sophomore with thick-framed tortoise-shell glasses, calls out to me, commanding my attention.

Willow is another member of the high school book club, so unsurprisingly, I see that she, too, has a Maisie book pushed to the side of her lunch tray.

I take a seat next to her, nervously eyeing the book. "Hi, Willow. That author sure has taken the school by storm, I suppose."

Willow chuckles. "More like the world. Have you seen the TikTok?"

I shake my head. "I'm not really a TikTok kind of girl."

Without pause, Willow pulls her phone from her pocket and scrolls to a video, pausing it before sliding it over to me. The woman on the screen can't be older than twenty-two. She has long brown hair falling over her shoulders in loose waves. She's wearing a bright pink lounge set, large turquoise glasses, and she's holding up a copy of Maisie's newest book, *Love On A Back Road.*

Seeing this stranger holding up my book causes my stomach to flip. I press the play button and listen intently as the girl speaks to her captive audience.

"Hey guys! I hope everyone is having the BEST Christmas break! I just wanted to pop on here real quick and tell you all about a new indie author I recently discovered, and I am totally obsessed with."

The girl pauses and quickly taps her long lavender-painted fingernails on the book cover. "This is *Love on a Back Road* by Maisie Bloomfield. I accidentally discovered Maisie one night while scrolling through Amazon, searching for a new book. Her bright, happy covers just called out to me, so I decided to take a chance on book one." She pauses dramatically. "When I tell you I devoured that entire book in one night, I am not even kidding. In fact, over the past three weeks, I have done basically nothing other than eat, sleep, and read Maisie Bloomfield books."

The woman pauses again and hugs the book tightly to her

chest. "These books have it all. Heart, humor, swoony men.... ugh. Chefs kiss. Literally. There's even a chef in one of them."

"Yeah, there is," Willow mutters with a smirk.

The brunette continues. "Maisie's books are closed-door, which means there's no on-page sex, but I promise you won't miss the steam because there's plenty of slow burn. Maisie has 15 books in her series, and I'm praying she doesn't stop anytime soon. I'm obsessed, and I've ordered every book because I know I'll read them over and over."

The girl places the book down on the table in front of her and leans in closer to the camera. "Okay, y'all. That's all for today. Go check out Maisie, buy all of her books. You won't regret it. Byeee!" The girl waves to the camera as the video loops to start over.

Willow closes the app and locks her phone, placing it on top of the book in question. "See?"

I shake my head. "Not really. I mean, that was a sweet review, but I have no idea how that translated to every female in Fawn Creek buying her books."

Willow chuckles. "Well, that was Riverly Austin."

I blink slowly. "I have no idea who that is."

"She's famous. Like super famous. She has over 2 million followers." Willow explains. "When she recommends things, people listen. And believe me, people listened."

The bell rings, signaling time to change classes, so I stand up from the cafeteria table. "Thanks for the insight, Willow. I'd better get to class."

Willow and I exchange our goodbyes, and I head down the main hall, back towards my classroom. The room is already half full of kids, but we have a few minutes before class starts.

Carefully, I open my laptop and log in to check my dashboard.

Honestly, I rarely check my sales; it's never mattered because I've always written for me and not for money. I never thought this would turn into anything lucrative. I love to teach, and I don't see myself ever stopping.

And I certainly never planned on going viral.

I click around the screen, viewing my sales for the month, and my mouth goes dry.

Today, I care. Because today I have reached over 1 million page reads, and I've sold hundreds of print copies. Today I've made over two thousand dollars in sales for the month, and it's only the 6th. Today, my little side hobby isn't looking all that hobby-like… and suddenly I realize I may have something to worry about after all.

Now that the world knows Maisie exists, how long can I keep myself separate from her?

I don't have much time to spend obsessing over sales and page reads, because it's time for class to start.

I close my laptop and look up to see a young boy with shaggy blonde hair standing in front of me.

"Hi," he greets me in a tone of voice that says he would rather be anywhere but here. "It's my first day. Where do I sit?"

"Hi. You're Corbin, right?" I ask.

I had an email this morning from the office reminding me of a new student starting today, but I met him before Christmas break. He and his dad were here at the end of school in December to finish his enrollment when Alex, her boyfriend, Noah, and I ran into them in the hall.

His dad, Dustin, grew up in Fawn Creek. He's older than me, so I don't remember much about him. I know he was your typical country boy. He spent his time hunting, fishing, and working on his pickup truck.

Dustin and Corbin moved to Fawn Creek over Christmas break to be closer to Dustin's family following the passing of Corbin's mom. When I met Corbin last month, he was not pleased with his father's decision. It looks like that hasn't changed much.

"Yep, that's me," he confirms. "Do you have assigned seats?"

I shake my head. "Nope, you can sit wherever." I pause for a second and lower my voice. "Do you want me to introduce you to the class?"

"Please no." Corbin groans. "I've had to introduce myself every hour so far. And I've been with 90% of the same kids over and over."

I nod. "You got it. I personally would rather eat a jean jacket than have to speak in front of a group of people, so I don't blame you at all."

My admission is enough to cause a slight smile to form on Corbin's face.

"Usually, no one sits in that desk right there," I say, pointing to a seat on the left side of the room. "Just in case you don't want to have a whole conversation with someone about why you're sitting in their seat, when no one has assigned seats in here."

"Thank you," Corbin whispers.

"Welcome. Did you bring a notebook that can stay in here?" I ask.

He nods.

"Good. Go ahead and have a seat."

I wait for Corbin to be seated before standing to address the classroom. "Okay, guys. You know the drill. Get your journals out and get ready for your writing prompt for the day."

The room is filled with groans from the kids, but they do as they are told, moving to get their journals from the shelf.

Everything is going to be just fine. I have to take it one day at a time.

* * *

I'm still reeling from the day as I step into Fawn Creek Market on the way home from work. Somehow, I'm not hungry at all, but I'm also starving and mildly afraid even to try to eat.

On days like today, I tend to stop by my parents' restaurant and get some comfort food. When I'm feeling overwhelmed, nothing in the world makes me feel better than a big bowl of mashed potatoes and gravy with a homemade roll.

But today, I can't even face my mom. As soon as I walk through those doors and sit down at the counter, she will know something is wrong. And she will not stop prodding until I at least make something up.

I may write fiction novels, but the idea of coming up with any fabrication actually exhausts me right now. Everything in my real life is exhausting right now.

What I need is a distraction from all the chaos that's going on around me.

My plan tonight is simple. I'm going to go home and lose myself in edits on my next book. Thankfully, the actual writing is done, because the way I'm feeling right now makes me want to never write again. And I hate that.

Writing has been my entire —secret— life for the last five years. And I don't think I'm ready to give it up just yet. I have to figure out how to keep it under wraps now that the entire world knows about Maisie.

I push my cart through the grocery store and make a beeline for a shelf of boxed mashed potatoes.

Don't tell my mom. She would never forgive me after all the years she spent teaching me how to perfect her mashed potato recipe. They are easily the best ones in Fawn Creek.

Just as I'm placing the box in my cart, a deep voice calls out my name.

Startled, I drop the box and turn towards the sound.

Why is my heart racing like I'm in trouble?

My eyes land on a familiar face, standing at the end cap. It's Dustin Crenshaw, Corbin's dad. And he is much too proud of himself for scaring the hell out of me.

I try to regain my composure. "Hi. How are you?"

His eyes dart to my cart and then back to me. "I'm great. But I'm worried about you. Does your mom know you're eating fake potatoes?"

I let out a heavy sigh. "No, and it's none of her business either. She doesn't control my potato intake. Not anymore, anyway."

He smirks. "Homemade is better."

I roll my eyes, as if I have this argument every day of my life. "That might be true, but have you ever tried making mashed potatoes for one person? It's too time-consuming, and since I'm not a potato snob, these will do just fine."

Dustin shrugs. "Carry on then, for what it's worth, Hamburger Helper is one of my favorite meals. I get made fun of all the time, but that, with some fake mashed potatoes on the side, has saved dinner more times than I could count. Especially in the past year, while I've tried to get a grasp on being a single parent. Corbin likes it, so that's all that matters to me."

"Speaking of Corbin. How was his first day?" I ask. "I had

him in my fifth hour, but I never had a chance to check in with him again before the day was over."

Dustin shrugs. "He's a teenager, that's for sure. Actually, you would probably have better luck getting information out of him than I do. I sent him a text at lunch to ask how it was going, and he just said: "Fine." I tried again after school and got a thumbs-up emoji.

I groan. "A thumbs up might as well be a finger emoji as far as teens are concerned."

He shakes his head, gently rolling his shopping cart forward. "Don't I know it."

I take a step towards him, softening my voice. "Well, for what it's worth, he seemed okay when I saw him this afternoon. I think he's going to do just fine here."

Dustin stares down at the ground, causing me to also look down at his dust-covered work boots and jeans with dried mud around the hem. "I hope you're right. Things haven't been easy since Karina died. I hope moving here was the right thing to do."

"I'm sure it was," I assure him. "He's just going to have to find his groove and make some friends. Once he does, it'll be easier."

"Making friends is going to be a tall order, I'm afraid," Dustin admits. "If he were interested in anything, it would be so much easier. He hates sports, and he can't play an instrument. He likes art, but there's no art club, just a class. Got any ideas?"

"Let me think about it. Many clubs meet at school. Surely there is something we can find that he will enjoy."

Dustin's shoulders seem to relax for the first time since we started talking, and a genuine smile appears on his lips. I can't help but notice a dimple on his cheek when he grins.

Either he's a lot cuter than I remember, or it's been too long since I've dated.

He pulls his wallet from his back pocket and hands me a business card. I run my finger over the raised font.

Dustin Crenshaw
Pipeline Supervisor

"Please," he says. "If you think of anything, shoot me a text. I think once he starts to get comfortable here, I can start to relax, too. Worrying about him is a full-time job, on top of my full-time job."

I flip the card over and study his phone number and email address before tucking it into my pocket. "I'll let you know what I come up with."

He smirks again. This time, it almost seems as though he's looking me up and down before he answers. "Thanks, Kristen. I appreciate the help, and if you ever need anything when it comes to Corbin, feel free to reach out to me anytime."

I swallow hard. His statement sounds more like an invitation than a request. Leave it to a rom-com author to find the romance in every interaction. I can almost see us making out on top of a pile of apples in the produce section.

But real life is nothing like the stories I write.

I need to get back in touch with reality. It has obviously been too long since I've kissed a man.

We exchange our goodbyes, and I watch as Dustin pushes his cart down the aisle, pausing to grab a box of Hamburger Helper along the way.

Suddenly, I feel inspired to write a new book. A book about a

teacher and a new blue-collar love interest...
And now, I can't wait to get home.

Chapter 4

I settle into my sofa with a large bowl of mashed potatoes and gravy. Jinx is snoozing at my side while my other two cats, Ash and Trip, are around here somewhere. They aren't quite the Velcro pets their little brother is.

While I eat, I pick up my phone and do something I swore I would never do.

I download TikTok.

Once the app is on my phone, I create an account, and I'm in.

I'm not here to like, comment, or interact. I'm here to see what exactly is going on with Maisie Bloomfield, and nothing else. I refuse to get sucked into a social media rabbit hole.

I locate the search bar and type *"Maisie Bloomfield"*. My eyes widen as the phone screen fills with videos of readers holding my... I mean Maisie's books. There have to be dozens upon dozens of them, which explains the sudden uptick in page reads and orders.

I click on the first video and settle in to watch as I eat my dinner. Over and over, readers rave about my books.

"These books changed my life."

"What a great palette cleanser in between dark romance reads."

"Maisie made me believe in love again."
Of course, there are a couple of people who don't love the stories as much as the others.
"Boring. This was too predictable."

"Where's the sex? I'd hoped there'd be sex!"

But for the most part. Maisie has a decent following and a much bigger fan base than I even imagined.

It's not hard to see how people get sucked into watching TikTok the way they do. Before I know it, my discarded mashed potato bowl is sitting on the wooden coffee table. I have a fur blanket across my lap, and I am easily thirty videos deep into my search.

That's when I notice a search prompt at the bottom of the screen.

Who is Maisie Bloomfield?

The words make my heart race, and immediately, my thoughts begin to spiral.

Does this mean this is what people are searching for? Is someone trying to find out who Maisie is? What if they figure it out?

I click through, and the app takes me to a suggested video. On the screen is a young lady; she can't be over the age of twenty. She has a stack of my books on the desk in front of her, and she is resting her chin on top of the stack.

"Unless you've been living under a rock," she begins with a smirk. "You've probably heard of Maisie Bloomfield. But, if you haven't, I'll fill you in. Maisie is an independent author who writes swoony, hilarious, and beautifully crafted small-town rom-coms. These books are relatable and sweet, and honestly, the best kind of palette cleanser for some of the spicier things that us Booktok girlies love. Maisie has a backlog of fifteen books and hopefully more on the way, so she has plenty of material to keep your mind entertained for a while. But, the real question is..." she leans forward slightly. "Who is Maisie Bloomfield?"

She pauses as though she's waiting for an answer before continuing. "Now there are a lot of theories out there. Maybe she's another highly prolific author who wanted to try a new genre under a different pen name. Or perhaps she is a housewife who's been dying to write books her entire life, but she doesn't want the PTA to know. Maybe she isn't even a she. Maybe Maisie is actually a man."

I groan. How are all of the rumors so very wrong? And why does it matter who I am anyway?

The girl continues. "She has no website. No social media accounts and no information on her Amazon author page. I think whoever Maisie is, she doesn't want to be found," she suggests with a shrug. "But what I do know is that wherever Maisie is, I imagine her life is just like her books. She's probably sitting at home right now, next to her husband, while they hold hands and dream about the future. Maybe they are lying on a blanket under the stars or snuggling in bed, reading books together. Wherever she is, I know that she is living a life full of happiness and romance. I'm sure she has found her happily ever after, and now she is just giving the rest of us hope. Thank you, Maisie, for the reminder that love is possible."

The video ends, and I close the app before turning to look at Jinx, who is stirring at my side. I gently scratch the top of his head, and he seems to smile up at me. "Oh buddy, they sure do have it wrong, don't they? For someone who writes so much about romance, my life is far from romantic."

Jinx meows in return and rubs his head against my thigh.

I stand from my seat and pick up my empty bowl. "You're right, buddy. There's no reason to sit here and feel all sad about the state of my life. We have a book to work on. If I'm going to continue to be a best-selling author, I need to get some words on paper. Especially now that my little grocery store run inspires me."

* * *

After my dishes are washed and I've had a shower, I put on another soft lounge-wear set — this one is a black jersey knit— and then I head into my office to start my evening job.

But tonight it feels different. All these years, I've been writing for me, Kristen. I've been trying to fulfill a childhood dream. There was nothing at stake.

But now? Now I have a very captive audience. And I don't want to let them down.

Of course, I've always known I've had readers. I've skimmed over my reviews from time to time, and they've been good. I've seen the sales, which have never been anything to write home about.

But, even so, I'm thankful now that I created an online bank account for my royalties to be deposited into.

In hindsight, the account was so I'd have a way to pay for editing services and writing expenses. I made sure it wasn't through my small-town bank because, even though the ladies who work there are wonderful, I didn't want to have to explain what I was doing.

Now, I'm thankful that no one will see a massive royalty deposit in a few months.

With the Maisie witch hunt that's happening online, I don't want to draw any unnecessary attention to myself. And a teacher with a random five-figure deposit from Amazon would most certainly raise an eyebrow or two.

I turn on my lamps, light my candle, and take a seat at my computer, powering it on. It opens directly to my current document, the one I'm supposed to be editing, so that it can be the next book in my series. But, instead, something is nagging at me —a new story.

A story of a teacher and a blue-collar man. A story of dirty jeans and work boots on the floor, next to her teacher's cardigan and teacher's bag. A story that feels a little bit close to home.

I don't have a deadline per se, well, unless you count the one that I put on myself. But nothing says that I can't take a break from edits and spend a little time writing something new while it's fresh on my mind, right?

I open a new document and take a deep breath, losing myself in the story that is playing over and over again in my head since walking out of the Fawn Creek Market.

For hours, I pound away on the keyboard. The click-clack of the keys sounds all through the house until late in the night.

To say tonight has been my best writing session ever is an understatement.

Usually, if I sit down and really focus for two hours, I can get around two thousand words on paper before I run out of steam and call it quits.

But something is different about this story. Instead of creating the characters, they seem to have created themselves. They are talking, living, and moving through this story, and I am merely a vessel for putting the words on the screen. And that's why I'm ending the night with just over four thousand words.

I stand to stretch my hands above my head and pause to look at the clock on my phone. I keep the clock hidden on my laptop on purpose. For the same reason, I keep my phone on do-not-disturb to limit distractions while I write.

It's two in the morning. My alarm will be going off in four hours. What have I done?

I'm going to need a lot of coffee to get through tomorrow.

Chapter 5

My alarm starts screaming at six in the morning, and I contemplate throwing my phone across the room. I'm not a morning person, no matter how hard I would love to be.

I hit the snooze button and lie in my bed, staring at the ceiling fan above my head.

I still can not believe I stayed up until after two writing this story, and I really can't believe that I could sit at my computer and easily write for another twelve hours right now. Honestly, my only motivation to get out of bed and start this day is so I can come home tonight and get back to work on my book.

It's going to be a very long day.

I start my coffee pot and get ready for the day, pulling on a long black tunic sweater, a pair of olive green skinny dress pants, and a pair of black Converse. I pull my shoulder-length black hair back with a claw clip and apply a little extra concealer to cover the bags under my eyes. The makeup does little to conceal the fact that I'm running on less than four hours of sleep, but it will have to do for now.

While I do my hair and makeup, I guzzle down two cups of coffee, but it's not nearly enough caffeine to wake me up or, even more importantly, get myself in the right state of mind.

But I have a job to do. So, I make the drive across town, offer

Sharon, the school secretary, a polite wave as I walk past the office, and practically crawl to my classroom.

I unload my teacher bag and start the coffee pot before sinking into my chair. There's still half an hour until school starts, and twenty-five minutes until students are going to start wandering in for the day.

Surely that's enough time for me to work on at least one of my books? I could work on edits; goodness knows I have plenty of them to work on. But that's not what I want to work on. I want to work on my new story. In fact, I need to.

I've never worked on a book at school before. In fact, that's why I made an office in my guest room, so I'd have a designated place to work on books without any interruptions. But would it really hurt to write one scene while waiting for the kids to come in?

I click on the document and place my hands on the keyboard just as the classroom door opens. It's Alex, the school librarian.

"Hey," she says, leaning into the room. She's wearing a red sweater over a white collared button-down shirt and black dress pants. Her large-framed glasses match her top perfectly, and long brown hair falls in loose waves over her shoulders, with her thick bangs landing just at the top of her glasses. "I haven't seen you since school started. I figured you'd pop into the library yesterday."

I causally close the document and turn towards my friend, attempting to conceal my panic from nearly being caught. "Yeah, sorry. I meant to, but yesterday was... weird."

Alex shrugs. "It's alright. Hopefully, today will be better. Hey, I just wanted to make sure you got the email about the book club selection? We are going to be reading the new book by Maisie Bloomfield."

I swallow hard and blink slowly.

Alex pauses, trying to read my response. "I know it's not your usual kind of read, but I hope you'll still join us, even if you don't read the book itself. It's good for us to get out of the house and have a life outside of school."

I nod. "Yeah, I'll pick up a copy and see what I can do," I promise her, knowing that this is going to be one book club meeting I'll skip.

Last fall, Alex talked to the owner of the downtown bookstore, and they had the idea of starting a book club. As much as I hate being dragged out of my house on a night off, to sit around with people I don't really know, I have to admit that it's been nice to form friendships with more bookish people.

Except for this next meeting. That's a hard no for me.

Listening to everyone gush over Maisie? Or even worse, listening to everyone talk about how much they hate my writing? Absolutely not. I will be faking being sick that day.

"You good?" Alex asks, still leaning against the door frame, studying my face.

I turn and catch a glimpse of myself in the mirror hanging next to the door. I look disgusted. Apparently, I'm so tired I forgot to turn off the subtitles on my face. Unfortunately, this is a regular occurrence for me.

"Yeah," I say, trying to play it off. "Just tired. I stayed up too late last night... reading."

It's only a half-lie. I did read back some of what I wrote.

Alex glances down at her watch and then back at me. She doesn't seem to be buying what I'm saying, but luckily, she's distracted. "Okay, if you say so. I'd better get the library opened for the day. Want to get together for lunch?"

I wince. There goes my plan to edit over my lunch break, so I can spend all night writing my new book. But, a break wouldn't hurt, right?

"Sure. My parents' place? Text me your order, and I'll go pick it up, and we can eat in the library."

She smiles, looking reasonably less concerned about me. "Perfect. See you soon."

I wait for Alex to leave and close the door behind her before turning my attention back to my computer.

That was close, too close probably.

Instead of trying to sneak in writing time on school property, I am better off leaving my romance writing for when I get home. No matter how hard this story is nagging at me, I do not need to get caught working as Maisie while dressed as Kristen. I have enough problems as it is.

* * *

I drag myself through the day until it's finally time for lunch. After a quick call to the restaurant to place my order, I jump in the car and head downtown. I even roll down my car window, letting the cool winter air wake me up a little.

As usual, downtown Fawn Creek is bustling with business. Even in a month like January, when sales are supposed to be slow and people are allegedly out of the house less, our town never seems to notice what the norm should be. That's the beauty of this town. People love supporting local businesses. No matter the time of year.

Somehow, I find an open parking spot near the diner among the work trucks and Cadillacs, before racing inside, leaving the engine running. This will only take a minute.

I push the glass door open, causing the bell above me to ring loudly, and I make my way into the diner. I take in the scene, one I've seen a million times already. My mom is standing at the checkout stand, cashing someone out. My dad is in the kitchen at the grill. The cutout that looks into the kitchen gives a clear view of his chest and his Red Maple T-shirt that he's wearing under his apron.

The tables are filled with customers of every kind; one holds a couple of moms, each with one toddler in tow, chatting over a plate of French fries while the kids watch a cartoon on the TV hanging on the wall. Another table holds an older couple who appear to be finishing up plates of turkey sandwiches and chips. Another table holds four chairs filled with men in tan button-down shirts and dirty work jeans.

I swallow hard. One of those men is very familiar. It's Dustin.

"Hey, Kristen," he calls out to me with a slight wave. "How's it going?

I swallow hard. "Hi," I reply, carefully.

I'm thankful that he can't read my mind. Otherwise, he would know that I was up all night writing a romance novel with a main male character based on him.

He definitely notices something is up. "Um, you good?"

"Yes, I'm fine. Totally fine." I answer quickly. "Sorry, I'm just tired. Um, I've got to grab my lunch and get back to work."

I offer him a slight wave and step towards my mom, who is holding a bag with my to-go order.

"Thank you," I say, taking the bag as I glance down to the counter next to the register and see a Maisie Bloomfield book, flipped open, page down.

Ugh, not her, too. I can't get away from Maisie to save my life. This is a nightmare.

Mom picks up the book and holds it up to show me. "Have

you read this?"

My eyes widen. I could say "Yes, actually a zillion times", but I lie.

"Nope, I sure haven't."

She frowns. "Well, you should. This might inspire you to find a man and get married finally. Maybe you can give me some grandbabies before I die."

With wide eyes, I look over my shoulder to see if Dustin is eavesdropping on us; luckily, he is not.

I lower my voice. "Greg already gave you grandbabies, remember?"

"You can never have too many."

"I highly doubt that's true," I reply. "Thank you for lunch. I love you."

"Love you," she replies, already with her nose buried in her book again.

I turn on my heel, glancing once more towards Dustin before making my way out the door and into the cool Kansas air. The wind hits my skin, and I suddenly realize I'm sweating. What in the world is going on with me?

* * *

I get back to the school and walk into the library, where Alex is sitting at a wooden table with her boyfriend, Noah, the gym teacher, across from her. I place the bag on the table and start to unpack my and Alex's lunch. I slide her container in front of her.

"Sorry, Noah. I would have ordered you something if I knew you were going to be here."

He shakes his head as Alex opens her Styrofoam container,

and he steals a fry. "Nope, don't worry about me. I'm not crashing your lunch and listening to the two of you yap about girl stuff."

I frown. "Girl stuff? So, you don't want to stay and chime in on a discussion of your favorite tampon brand?"

Noah sighs loudly. "No thanks," he says, making his way towards the door.

"But, Noah! We were going to take a poll on how the brands vary from light to heavy days." I call out to him, grinning at the look of terror on his face.

Man, I forgot how fun it is to terrorize men with period talk. I miss my brother.

Alex shakes her head and takes a seat across from me. "Poor guy," she says, looking out at the doorway where her boyfriend had just made his narrow escape.

I wave her off. "He's tough. He's going to be okay."

Alex smirks in response as she picks up her BLT and pauses before taking a bite. "I'm sure you're right. Well, how's it going getting back into the swing of things?"

"I'm fine," I reply quickly, in a rush to get the conversation off me. "Let's talk about you. How was your Christmas with your new boyfriend? How was it with your family? Did they approve?"

Alex smiles widely, and her face blushes slightly. It's clear she is head over heels in love with our doofy gym teacher.

"They loved him, and he loved them. It was actually a perfect Christmas with my family. Hopefully, next year we can have my family and his come to our house and spend Christmas together."

I smirk. "So, you're moving in together."

"No, not yet," Alex argues, "but by next year, I'm sure I will be living there. I want to make sure I don't rush into anything. But, I'm happy." Alex pauses to study my face. "So, all we need now is for you to find a great guy, too."

I toss a fry into my mouth. "Great guys don't exist."

"Noah exists."

I shrug. "And he's taken. Guess my mom was right. I'm destined to die alone."

Alex rolls her eyes at my joke. "No, you are not going to die alone. The right one is out there, and you'll find him. I'm sure of it."

I guess at least someone has faith in me.

Alex and I are just finishing up our meal when Hannah, one of our favorite substitute teachers, pokes her head into the room.

"Hey, girls!" she greets us in a perky voice. "How's it going?"

Hannah is adorable and has the best fashion sense. She has long, blonde hair that she wears in springy curls, and she tends to always dress in loose, flowy dresses, linen pants, or fun overalls. She's just so whimsical, and honestly, she almost makes me want to add a little color to my wardrobe. Almost.

Today, she's wearing linen pants with a graphic T-shirt. The shirt features a goose holding an umbrella and wearing rain boots. The words around the image say, *You guys go ahead. I'm going to dilly dally.*

"Hey, Hannah," Alex greets her with a smile. "Who are you subbing for today?"

Hannah leans back, taking a seat on the edge of the table behind her. "Art. In fact, you two are looking at the official long-term sub for the Art Department. I'll be here for the rest of the year."

Alex claps her hands together in excitement. "Oh, yay, you'll be great in there. You're so creative, and the kids love it when you sub."

I pick up a fry and dip it in my ranch. "But, wait. What happened to Marge?"

"Oh, I guess word hasn't gotten around yet," Hannah shakes her head. "Marge is taking early retirement. She got hurt on a cruise over Christmas break, and she's going to have hip surgery. Her recovery is going to be a long one, and she decided she might as well retire at this point."

"Man, those cruise ships are dangerous. You wouldn't catch me dead on one of those." I shake my head.

Alex shrugs. "I don't know. I think a cruise could be fun. Maybe I'll talk you into one someday," she tells me with a smirk, before turning back to Hannah. "But, anyway, welcome to Fawn Creek High, Hannah. I think you'll do great. Maybe you'll love it so much that you can take over the Art Department permanently."

"Gerald is already all over that," Hannah admits. "I told him we are just going to see how it goes."

"Yep, you're officially stuck. Welcome to the rest of your life. Once you get in, you can't get out." I warn her before softening my voice a bit. "But, there really are worse places to work. You should consider it."

She nods. "I might."

That's when an idea hits me. "Hey, any chance you might want to start an after-school art club? I have a new kid with a dad who is very concerned about him finding an extracurricular activity. It's like one of the few boys in Southeast Kansas who doesn't want to go out for sports."

Hannah shakes her head no, with zero hesitation. "Absolutely not. At least not this year. It's going to be hard enough to balance working full-time for the first time since my son was born. I can't take on anything extra quite yet."

I nod. "I get it. And I don't blame you. I just told his dad I'd try to think of something for him."

Hannah nods. "Is it Corbin Crenshaw?"

"Yep," I confirm. "He's had kind of a rough year, and I just want to help him get adjusted."

"He seems like a great kid. And he's very talented, from what I've seen so far." Hannah shrugs. "I wish I could help."

I shake my head. "It's okay. I'll figure out something."

Chapter 6

After lunch, I get back to my classroom, retrieve Dustin's business card, and fire off a text to let him know that art club was a no-go.

Kristen: Hey, it's Kristen Calhoun. I just wanted to let you know that I tried to revive the art club today, but I didn't have any luck. I'll keep trying to find him something to get involved in, though.

Dustin replies almost immediately.

Dustin: Hey, thanks for trying. And thanks for thinking of me.

My face immediately grows warm, and I know I'm blushing like an idiot. If only he knew how much I have been thinking about him since last night.

Kristen: No problem. I'll keep looking, and I'll keep you in the loop.

Dustin: Looking forward to it.

I read the text and pause for a second to analyze his words. That almost seemed flirty... didn't it? I mean, he could have just said thanks. Why'd he mention that he's looking forward to hearing from me again?

Or maybe I'm reading into this too much after staying up all night writing a love story with him as the main character. It's probably that one.

I'm officially delusional.

I move through the rest of the day without too much excitement. Just as I'm packing up for the day during the last few minutes of eighth hour, an announcement comes over the school PA system. It's Sharon.

"Students and staff, this is just a reminder that the high school scholars bowl meeting has been scheduled for Friday after school," she says, sounding as though she is reading from a note or a teleprompter.

That's when the idea occurs to me. Scholar's Bowl. That's the perfect fit for a kid like Corbin. He's smart. He's only been here for a couple of days, but his assignments and journal entries have proved that much already. Plus, this would give him the perfect team to join without having to pretend to be interested in sports.

I pick up my phone and fire off a text to Dustin.

Kristen: Hey, new idea. What about Scholar's Bowl? I think that would be a great fit for Corbin. A couple of the boys that I've seen him talking to at school are already involved. And don't worry, they are good kids.

I watch as the three dots bounce on the phone screen as he types a response. Is he writing a novel? Shockingly, it's a short response.

Dustin: Great idea. When do they meet?

Kristen: Friday at three.

Dustin: I'll talk to him tonight and get back to you... Thanks for all your help. I owe you.

Oh, Dustin, don't worry. You've already helped plenty through inspiration.

* * *

After yet another long night of tapping away at my keyboard, but this time setting an alarm so I quit at a respectable time, I roll out of bed and head into school ready for another day.

The day passes smoothly with the kids falling back into a steady rhythm as we head into the second semester. I've almost forgotten about the fact that my life is teetering on the edge of explosion when Gerald Holeman, the high school Principal, pops into my room during my planning period. I'm sitting at my desk with a cup of coffee in front of me as I grade papers when he steps into the room.

"Ms. Calhoun. I'm so glad I caught you," he says, stepping towards my desk.

As far as bosses go, Gerald is one of the best. He's a kind man who treats all the staff members like people, rather than just a nameplate on a desk. And that goes for everyone. He knows that teachers and admin are just as important as janitors and cafeteria workers, and he treats everyone accordingly.

He has one of the best laughs, which causes his round belly to bounce all over the place when you really get him going. But he is also no stranger to hard work, and he expects the rest of the building to feel the same way.

Which is why I try hard to fight the frown that is begging to show on my face when he comes looking for me. Unfortunately, if Gerald is seeking me out for anything, it's not going to be good or make my life any easier.

I place my red ink pen down on the pile of papers and look up to give him my full attention. "What can I do for you, Gerald?"

He pauses, sitting lightly on the student desk behind him, being careful not to put all of his weight on the furniture. "Well, this isn't so much about what you can do for me, but what you can do for the children, Ms. Calhoun."

Oh gosh, here we go with the guilt trip.

He continues. "As I'm sure you know, the Scholar's Bowl team is set to have its first meeting of the semester this Friday."

I nod.

"And, I'm not sure if you've heard, but Marge Baker, the woman who has been acting as the coach for several years now, has had to take an unexpected leave of absence."

I nod. "I have heard a little bit. Is Marge okay?"

He frowns. "It's a shame, really. She went on one of those Caribbean Cruises with her family over the holidays. It was supposed to be all sunshine and happiness, but instead, Marge had one too many Piña Coladas and went a little too wild in the club."

I hold my hand to my chest, as though I'm clutching my pearls. "Marge! Dang. I didn't know she had it in her."

Gerald chuckles softly, "I don't think she knew either. Anyway, like I said, she popped it and locked it a little too hard on her trip. I'm afraid she is going to be out for the rest of the year due to an upcoming hip surgery. She will be taking an early retirement at the end of the year."

I shake my head, picturing old Marge in a tropical floral mumu dancing in the night club on a cruise ship with a Piña Colada in one hand. And then work really hard to not laugh at the image in my head before looking back at my boss. "I'm so sorry that happened to her, but Gerald, what does that have to do with me?"

He smiles gently, "Well, I was hoping that I could persuade you to take over for Marge."

I scrunch my nose. "In the art room? I mean, I'm already kind of busy teaching English. And I thought Hannah had that covered?"

He holds up his hands and waves them. "No, of course not. Hannah has the Art Department under control for the remainder of the year. What I need is someone who can take over coaching the Scholar's Bowl team."

And there it is.

"Oh."

"And I think you would be an excellent fit," he continues. "In fact, I would dare to say that you are made for a job like this."

I shake my head. "I'm not really the coaching type. And I really don't know the first thing about coaching Scholar's Bowl."

"That's the beauty of it all, Ms. Calhoun. The kids already know what they are doing. It's a good group, honestly— a real bright team. And they have a real chance of winning at State this year. They need an adult who can drive the van to get them to the tournaments."

I frown. "And you can't do it because?"

Gerald clears his throat. "Well, I can't help because I'm already stretched pretty thin with the boy's basketball team."

I take a deep breath and settle back into my seat. "I don't know Gerald. I'm not sure I have the time available."

"Think of the kids. We even have a new boy joining the team, Corbin Crenshaw. I just spoke to him this morning about joining. That kid has had a pretty rough year and could really use a team and some friends to connect with." He pauses for a second, as though to really drive the point home. "Unfortunately, I have asked everyone, and if you can't help me out, then the team will have to disband."

Dammit. He got me. I was the one who suggested Corbin join in the first place, and if I don't step into this position, he's back to square one. And so is Dustin.

"Fine," I groan, against my better judgment. "I'll do it."

Gerald grins, clearly celebrating his victory. "Great. The team meets on Friday after school. This will be a great opportunity for you to really get to know the kids before heading off to the state tournament in Manhattan next month."

I raise a brow. "Manhattan? So we are going to have to travel and stay the weekend?"

"Yes, of course," he answers as though this is something I should have known. "I'll have Sharon send over the list of students so that you can talk to the parents about accommodations. I'm sure it won't be a problem to find at least one other parent to join you and help supervise at the hotel.

I nod, swallowing hard as I try to make sense of these new obstacles. "Okay, yes, please pass that along. I want to get that sorted out sooner rather than later."

Gerald stands and makes his way towards the door before

turning to look back at me. "Thanks again, Kristen. I knew we could count on you."

He disappears, and I lay my head down on my desk, talking to my feet. "Oh, you know me. Ms. Reliable... more like Ms. No Life Who Can't Say No When It Comes To These Kids."

And definitely one kid in particular.

* * *

"So, wait a second. *You* are the new coach of the scholars' bowl team?" My dad clarifies.

I'm sitting at an empty booth in the diner, rolling silverware while he sits across from me, finishing the nightly deposit. I shrug. "Yep, seems that way."

He chuckles softly. "I didn't know you were interested in Scholar's Bowl enough to become a coach."

I band the silverware roll in my hand and add it to the growing pile. "Well, that makes two of us."

"You regret it yet?"

I shake my head. "No, not really. I mean. Maybe I'll do it and love it. Maybe I'll do it for the year and then tell him I'm out for next year."

"Ha!" Dad barks out a laugh. "Kid, you know as well as I do this is not the kind of position you can just walk away from. The only way to get out of something like this is to die or move away. And as your father, I don't permit you to do either of those. I mean, who would cover shifts for the wait staff when they have to cheer at the basketball game?"

"I'm sure you'd find someone else," I say, rolling my eyes. "I can't do this forever, you know."

"We wouldn't find anyone like you, Kid." He smirks. "And

I'm sure that's why they asked you to help out. You do a great job, and those kids respect you. I hear it from my employees all the time."

I shrug, finishing my job as Mom walks into the room. "I don't know. I wonder if they asked me because they can count on me to have nothing else going on in my life. That's what I get for being a single thirty-year-old with no kids."

Mom takes a seat at the counter and turns to join our conversation. "Well, you could change that by getting married."

I stand from my seat and stretch. "Well, shoot. I didn't even think of that. Are you going to need me tomorrow, because if not, I think I'll see if I can get me a mail-order husband and solve all my problems."

Dad chuckles, and Mom lets out a heavy sigh. "That's not what I meant," she groans.

I move towards my mother and wrap my arms around her. "I know. And I know you mean well. It's just not my turn yet."

"Your time is coming, sweet girl. I know it," she promises me.

"Thanks, Mom," I smirk. "Well, if you two are done with me, I'm going to head home. I have some things to finish up before bed."

"Night, kiddo." Dad smiles. "Thanks for coming to help tonight."

"Anytime. Love you, guys."

"Love you, too," Mom says, following me to the door to lock it behind me. "Don't stay up all night grading papers."

"I won't," I promise.

But I can't make any promises about staying up all night writing my newest love story.

Chapter 7

The week flies by, and before I know it, it's Friday afternoon and almost time for our first Scholar's Bowl meeting. At three o'clock, the bell rings, and my last hour kids trickle out of my room. By 3:05, I have six kids sitting in various desks around the room. There are four boys— Corbin, Jaxson, Nash, and Dillon—and two girls, Kaci and Heather.

"Is this everyone?" I ask, taking a seat at my podium in the front of the room. On my desk sits the buzzer box and the box of questions Gerald dropped off this morning, but we have some other business to take care of first.

The kids glance around at each other and then nod in unison.

I clap my hands together. "Perfect, let's get started. So, I think the first order of business is the state tournament. It looks like it'll be the second weekend of February, which means that we have about a month to get things sorted out."

Just as I finish speaking, someone walks through the door, catching my eye. At first, I assume it's another student coming to join the team, but it's an adult.

It's Dustin. He offers a quiet wave.

"Sorry, I'm late."

I furrow my brow and open my mouth, but Corbin chimes in before I can say anything.

Corbin groans and sinks in his seat. "Seriously? Why are you here?"

Dustin's face reddens, and he turns to his son. "I'm sorry. I didn't know this wasn't a parent thing. I just thought... I don't know. I used always to go to practice when you played soccer."

Corbin replies through gritted teeth. "I was five. You had to be there because you had to drive me."

I step between the two to de-escalate the situation.

"Listen, I'm sorry. This is my fault." I lie. "I asked your dad to come help since I have never run a Scholars Bowl practice before."

I turn towards the out-of-place dad to further prove my point. "Thank you so much for coming. You're a lifesaver. You can have a seat back there." I point towards the last row of desks.

Dustin smirks and mouths a "thank you" to me before wedging himself into a desk at the back of the room. I try not to snicker at the image of a fully grown man scrunched into the seat. He stretches his legs out in front of him since he has no room to bend them under the desk. That can't be comfortable.

"Anyway," I continue. "Like I was saying, we need to figure out the logistics of the trip to State. It's the second week of February, and it's in Manhattan. The tournament starts at eight in the morning. I would love to drive up there the day before and stay the night, so we aren't making the drive at three in the morning."

"Makes sense," Kaci, a senior with long dark hair, replies. "That's what we usually do."

I nod. "And usually, you have Marge and her husband, but this time you just have me. I can room with the girls, but we need a dad to room with the boys."

"I'll do it," Dustin chimes in while simultaneously shooing his hand into the air.

"Dad, you don't have to raise your hand to talk," Corbin mutters. "This isn't school."

Dustin's face turns a deep red. "Sorry, I guess the desk made me nostalgic. I'm fighting the urge to pop my back in this thing."

I shrug. "I do it all the time. It's one of the perks of the job. I don't have time to go to the doctor, so I am my own chiropractor."

Heather chimes in. "As long as you aren't your own gynecol—"

"Stop right there," I shout, holding up a hand towards Heather, cutting her off before she can continue the word.

Heather grins, looking entirely too proud of herself.

Dustin snickers to himself, and I wish I could hide under a desk.

I swear, you never know what's going to come out of a teenager's mouth, but these kids always seem to know how to toe the line of what is appropriate or not.

"Anyway," I reply loudly, "Dustin, did you have something to say?"

Dustin clears his throat. "Yeah. Um, I was saying that I volunteer to come on the trip. I can do a background check or whatever you need."

I nod, and my eyes dart to Corbin. He shrugs as though to permit me to let his dad join us. "Perfect. That would be great. Thank you."

He smirks, "Anytime."

That sounded flirty. *Is he flirting with me in front of the kids?*

No. He's not flirting. He's just an involved dad. Just because

I've been sitting at home writing a romance novel with him as the main male character all week does not mean he feels the same about me.

Right?

"So," Kaci chimes in, standing from her seat. "Are we ready to practice?"

Her question snaps me back to reality. "Yes, almost," I reply quickly. "I will have permission slips for your parents. We will leave that Friday, probably during seventh hour, and we will be taking the school van. Any questions?"

"Who is driving?" Dillon, a sophomore boy, asks.

"Me."

He frowns. "Do you know how to drive the van?"

I grit my teeth. "Yes, Dillon, it will be fine. I've driven it dozens of times. And I even have a certificate around here somewhere that says I'm competent."

"Okay..." he responds, but he still looks concerned.

"Anyway, I know that only about two of you will remember to relay this information to your parents so that I will send out an email tomorrow with all the information, as well as a packing list. Now, what do you guys do during these meetings?"

Kaci speaks up again. "I'm the team captain. We usually practice for about an hour. I'll set up the buzzer box, and Ms. Calhoun, you read the questions to us. There's a shoe box full of index cards over by the buzzer box. Corbin's dad, you can keep score on the whiteboard."

"You guys can call me Dustin," Dustin answers, taking his position in front of the board. "And you've got it."

The kids shuffle the desks around the room, then split into two teams and gather around the buzzer box. When they are in place, I pull out my first question card.

"Alright, team, let's start with your favorite subject, Literature," I announce with a grin. "Name the author of the novel, 'To Kill A Mockingbird'.

Corbin buzzes in before I can even finish asking the question. "Harper Lee".

"Correct," I nod, "One point for Team A."

Dustin marks a point under the heading for Team A and gives Corbin an enthusiastic thumbs up. Corbin's face turns a shade of deep red.

I make a mental note to talk to Dustin later. If he doesn't want Corbin to kill him before the trip to Manhattan, he is going to have to tone it down just a bit.

The next thirty minutes are a blur as the teams battle it out, and I read off questions over everything from the Louisiana Purchase to the Periodic Table.

Finally, the clock on the wall tells me it's almost four and time to wrap things up.

"Okay, guys, last question. Who painted the Mona Lisa?"

Both teams buzz in at the same time, but Team B, Kaci's team, is ahead by maybe half a second. Jaxson is the first one to hit the buzzer.

"Leonardo da Vinci," he answers proudly.

I give Dustin the nod, and he marks the final point on the board with a flourish.

"Alright, Team B. You officially have bragging rights for the next week. Go ahead and put the desks back where they go, and you guys can go. I'll get that email sent out to your parents tomorrow."

The kids get to work on cleaning up the classroom, and Dustin follows me back to my desk.

"Well, we make a pretty good team, don't we?" Dustin says,

sitting on the corner of my desk. He has a smug grin on his face, and I can't help but notice the hem of his sleeve riding up his muscular bicep.

Yowza, I never realized how attracted to biceps I am. That's going in the book for sure.

His question catches me off guard. "I'm sorry, what?"

He grins softly. "You and I," he answers and then pauses. "I mean, all of us really. I think we will do great at the state tournament."

I lower my voice, "About that."

He frowns. "You don't want me to come?"

The pointed question causes me to swallow hard. "No. Yes." I stutter. "Actually, let's start over. Yes, I do want you to come with us. We honestly can't do it without you. It's just, you might want to take the enthusiasm down a notch if you want Corbin not to murder you between now and then."

Dustin removes his hat and runs a hand through his hair. "It was the thumbs up, wasn't it?"

I nod. "Oh yeah."

Dustin looks back at Corbin, who is lost in conversation with Jaxson. "I knew it was too much as soon as I did it, but it was too late. I can't help it. That kid is so smart. I'm so proud of him, and seeing him be a part of something new like this makes me even more proud."

I smile gently and reach out to pat his shoulder. But when I touch him, I regret it instantly.

It's like a spark of electricity shoots from his shoulder to my hand and straight to my stomach.

Ugh. I've got it bad.

I pull back quickly and try to play it cool.

"Hey, I get it. He is a smart kid, and I've enjoyed getting to know him and watching him come out of his shell. But, if you are going to be involved in school stuff, which I believe you should be, very few high school parents are, you are going to have to play it cool."

He steps closer to me and leans in. "I have never been one to be good at playing it cool."

The sound of his confession sent chills up my spine. I try to respond, but I can't speak.

"You'll have to help keep me in line," he adds.

Oh my gosh.

If only he knew the words I'll be putting on paper this weekend, thanks to him.

* * *

After a quick stop to pick up a pizza and a bottle of wine, I make my way home. The plan for the weekend is clear. I need to finish the edits on book sixteen, Love on the Prairie, and then I can fully lose myself in writing my story about a sexy blue-collar worker and a schoolteacher.

This new book is quickly becoming my favorite story I've ever written, and I'm sure that it's because, for once, the book is inspired by my own life. However, I really need to finish the one I'm working on before I really immerse myself.

I eat, shower, and then change into my lounge clothes before unlocking the door to the pink room and settling into my chair.

Jinx settles into my lap and falls asleep in seconds.

And of course, I have no desire to work on edits.

I want to write a story of a sexy blue-collar man with ripped biceps and the teacher who wishes she could tear his shirt off to expose the rest of him.

I set a timer for an hour to work on edits, but, per usual, I find myself bored and distracted as I make the corrections my editor sent. I add commas and change words, but at a snail's pace.

Finally, I force myself to finish edits on two chapters, make another cup of coffee, and then dive into my story, the story that is suddenly feeling very, very real.

With one move, he picks me up by my waist and places me down on the desk. Before I can even think twice about the difference between right and wrong, he leans down, and his lips meet mine. My hands run through his hair as I steady him, keeping him pulled in close to me.

Finally, he pulls back to take a breath and rests his forehead on mine. "I've been waiting to do that for a long time," he admits.

"I've been waiting for you to do that for a long time," I reply as I try to steady my breathing.

"Do you want to take this back to my place?" he asks, just above a whisper, before leaning in to gently kiss my neck.

I pull back. "We need to take it somewhere, or I'm going to be without a job when we get caught doing it here."

I finish writing the scene and lean back into my chair to read it over. No matter how many stories I've written, there is something about this one that is different.

It's fiction. None of this has happened, but it still feels real. Or maybe, deep down, it's because it's something I wish could happen.

Chapter 8

Thanks to a weekend off work and plenty of motivation, I fly right through my to-do list. By Sunday afternoon, the only thing I have left to work on is my newest book.

Edits are done for *Love on the Prairie.* My house is clean, my laundry is put away, and I have officially gotten to work on my newest book, *Lessons in Love.*

Of course, writing this story doesn't actually feel like work at all. In fact, this book is practically writing itself. It almost seems as though the words are coming to me faster than I can get them down on my computer screen.

Over time, I've become a creature of habit when it comes to writing. I have my routine of settling into my office, lighting my candle, turning on my lamp, and sipping hot tea while I write, maybe 1,500 words a day. On a good day, if I really try, I can get 2,000 words, but those days are few and far between. By the time I'm inching towards 2,000 words, I generally get tired and a little bored.

But this story is different.

Suddenly, I am easily churning out 2,500 to 3,000 words a day. If I didn't have to pull myself away from my computer to work, shower, and sleep, I'm sure I could put out even more.

Honestly, I could probably write this entire book in half the time it usually takes me to complete a story.

The main characters, Darren and Katie, seem to be running the show when it comes to writing. I've never been much of an outliner. I like to let my characters tell me what's going to happen next, but I usually have a general idea of what will happen.

Not with this one, though.

With this story, I sit down, place my hands on the keyboard, and see where they take me. Let me say, it's been a wild ride.

I write for a couple of hours and only take a break because Ash is standing next to my chair, meowing at the top of her lungs. She must be out of food; that's about the only time she wants anything to do with people.

"Okay, okay. Let's get some dinner," I assure her, as the two of us race towards the empty cat food bowls in the dining room. The clatter of dry cat food hitting the three metal bowls draws the other two cats running. Before I can even finish portioning out their dinner, all three cats are feasting dramatically as though they haven't eaten in months.

With the animals being fed, it only makes sense to take a break and have dinner as well.

I throw some leftover pizza in the microwave and check my phone for the first time in hours.

It's been on Do Not Disturb for a couple of hours while I've been writing. Usually, I don't get bothered too much by the outside world. I'm not very active on social media, so notifications from there are few and far between.

I have a couple of emails from companies offering me Valentine's Day sales, and one text, it's from Dustin.

Dustin: Hey. I just overheard Corbin and Jaxson talking while

they were playing a video game. I guess Jaxson said they had matching shirts to wear to State last year. Any idea where I can get a shirt for Corbin?

I pause for a second, considering his question. I suppose I could text Marge and see if we have any extras lying around. But I also don't hate the idea of ordering new shirts for everyone. The last time I saw Dillon walking the halls in his, it had a hole in it and a stain that I can only imagine came from spaghetti day in the cafeteria. I'm pretty sure the kids have been wearing those same shirts for years.

Kristen: You know, maybe it's time to think about ordering new shirts for the team. I know a girl in town, Avery, who can make them for us. The old ones are pretty outdated. I'm sure it wouldn't be too expensive to have them printed. Maybe the kids would even like to help design them.

Dustin: I'd be happy to cover the cost of the shirts. Just let me know how much you need.

I read his text and smile to myself. Man, it's really hard to ignore how much I like this guy, especially when he offers things like this.

Truly, it's not about the money. The cost won't be much, and for the most part, I know the parents will have no problem buying their kids new shirts. And if one of the kids couldn't get the money together, I would have paid for their shirt so they didn't have to go without.

The reason why I find Dustin's offer so endearing is just for the simple fact that he's willing to help. Parents are busy as it is. They are juggling careers, housework, their kids' activities, and life in general. God forbid they try to fit a social life, or hobbies, or anything else into their schedule. It's a lot. Even I know that, and I don't have kids.

To top it off, Dustin's a single dad. Sure, he has his mom and dad to help out, but at the end of the day, all of the parenting concerns are on his shoulders.

Because of things like this, I never expect high school parents to offer their time, and raising kids is expensive, so I don't really expect them to throw around money either.

But Dustin's different. He sees what needs to be done, and he does it. He doesn't stop and think about it. He takes care of business. The world needs more people who are willing to pitch in. The world could always use more helpers.

Kristen: That's really nice of you. You don't have to do that.

Dustin: I'm happy to help. Just think of all the money I've saved during Corbin's lifetime by not having to pay for expensive sports equipment that he'd probably lose or outgrow within a month. Get me one, too? Size Large.

Kristen: You got it. Thanks again for your help.

I put my phone down on the counter, assuming our conversation is over, and pick up my slice of pizza. But another message comes across the screen.

Dustin: It's the least I could do after you covered for me when I crashed practice Friday. Actually, I think I owe you pretty big for that one. Why don't you let me take you out for dinner

sometime, so I can really show you my appreciation?

I read the text and swallow hard, battling the lump in my throat. So, I wasn't imagining it, was I? He really was flirting with me. I was just too dense to see it. I bite my lip and type a message back on the screen, hitting send before I get a chance to change my mind.

Kristen: Sure, I'd like that.

I put my phone back down and pause to take in the moment. Is the story in my head becoming my reality?

* * *

By lunchtime on Monday, I've already sent an email to the Scholar's Bowl kids asking them to come up with ideas for shirt designs, and I've messaged Avery, the local mobile boutique owner/T-shirt maker, to make sure she can take care of us. She assured me that she could fix us up in just a few days.

We will have the shirt issue handled on Friday and get her the order with plenty of time to spare. The kids, apparently, have other plans.

At the end of the day on Monday, I'm getting ready to leave after school when Kaci bursts into my classroom. She has the entire Scholar's Bowl team on her heels.

I glance around at the eager kids standing in my room and blink slowly. Do I have the day wrong? Did I black out and miss an entire week of my life?

"Guys, we don't have a meeting today. That's Friday."

"I called an emergency meeting," Kaci replies.

"You can't do that," I tell her.

"I already did, obviously," she shrugs, with way more audacity than a seventeen-year-old girl should possess. "We've got to talk about this T-shirt thing."

I nod, slowly lowering myself back into my seat. I'm not going to be getting out of here anytime soon. "I know. That's why I sent out a group email, so that we could discuss it in there and finalize things on Friday."

"That's what I said," Jaxson groans.

Kaci lifts a brow; she is obviously very passionate about this meeting that could have been an email. "Listen, I'm the team captain, and I think we all need to be on the same page when it comes to these shirts. We don't want to look like a group of dorks when we are at State."

"We literally are dorks," Nash tells her. "What do you think Scholar's Bowl kids are? A group of nerds."

I frown. "Listen, I wouldn't go that far." I've never been a fan of stereotypes, especially with teens who are just figuring out who they are. They don't need to be put in any more boxes than they already are.

"I would go that far." Dillon chimes in. "But, it's fine. My mom told me that it's okay to be nerdy."

Kaci blinks slowly. "You know, that's just stuff that moms say so a kid doesn't feel insecure about not being cool, right?"

"Rude," Heather mutters under her breath.

"It's true,' Kaci retorts.

"Okay, that's enough." I hold up a hand, stepping in. "Well, Kaci, you obviously have some very strong feelings about the shirt design, so you must have an idea."

Kaci straightens where she stands. "Yes, I think we should go with something casual. Like a pair of glasses, and then underneath it, it can say something like *Keep Calm and Buzz In?*"

The kids all go silent, exchanging glances but not speaking.

Kaci looks around at the team. 'Well, what do you guys think?"

"Eh," Heather speaks up first. "It's kinda basic. Don't you think?"

Kaci nods. "Basic is fine. Then we will be able to wear them again when the season is over."

"Oh my gosh, Kaci. Where are you going to wear a shirt that says *Keep Calm and Buzz In?*" Nash asks, his hands planted firmly on his hips.

Kaci groans. "I don't know. Everywhere?"

"Maybe to do lawn work," Jaxson chimes in.

I look around the room, my eyes landing on Corbin, who has quietly gotten into his backpack and pulled out his Chromebook. He is waiting patiently for the arguing to end while he sits on the top of a desk, slowly swinging his legs back and forth.

We make eye contact, and he sends me a forced smile.

"Corbin, do you have an idea?" I ask, hoping I'm not calling him out for no reason.

He nods. "Yeah. I just made this earlier today. It's probably stupid but..." With that, he spins the computer around for us to take a look. The screen features a Prairie Dog, the school mascot, wearing a red sweater with FCHS in large letters across the front. Around the top of the Prairie Dog are the words "Fawn Creek Scholar's Bowl."

Heather's the first to speak. "He's wearing a tiny sweater."

"That's a shirt I'd wear in public." Jaxson chimes in. "Plus, no one is going to have one like that. We will stand out from everyone else."

I step forward. "Okay, let's take a vote. First, Kaci's idea?" I pause, looking out across the kids.

No one raises a hand. Sorry Kaci.

"And Corbin's idea?"

Every hand raises... even Kaci's.

I scan the room, counting hands, and then turn to face the team. "Okay, I think that settles it. "Corbin, email that over to me. Everyone, send me your shirt sizes. And we all agree on black shirts with a white design?"

The kids all nod in agreement.

"Can you ask Avery if she can give the Prairie Dog a red shirt?" Kaci chimes in.

"Absolutely." I agree, "and Corbin's dad covers the cost of the shirts, so you guys do not have to come up with any money."

"Nice," Dillon chimes in, as he picks up his bag. "Okay, my mom is sitting outside and is probably ready to kill me. I gotta go."

I groan. "Go. Tell her I'm sorry. And the rest of you go, too. I need to get home. Don't forget to send me your sizes by tomorrow morning. And no more surprise meetings. I have a life outside of school, too, you know."

"You do?" Dillon asks, not bothering to hide the look of confusion on his face. "Since when?"

I let out a heavy sigh. "Bye. Have a good night."

Chapter 9

"Thank you so much, Avery. I'll get that file sent over to you now." My phone is cradled between my ear and my shoulder while I stand at the stove, browning a pan of hamburger meat. "We really appreciate you being able to do these for us."

"It's no problem at all," she promises. "I'll get the order placed as soon as I get the file. Looks like everything should be here by Wednesday, so you should be able to pick them up at TBR on Thursday after work."

I pause, counting the days on my fingers. Three days. "That's... incredibly fast. A lot faster than I was expecting."

Avery chuckles. "Well, besides juggling the twins and Juliet, this is my full-time job now, so I have much faster turnaround times than I used to."

I shake my head as though she can see me. Then, I leave the pan simmering on the stove and move towards my laptop. "I don't know how you juggle three kids and a business. I can barely juggle three cats and a job." I email her the file and move back towards my cooking.

"It was touch and go there for a while, but we've finally fallen into a steady rhythm," Avery admits, with the sound of tapping on the keyboard in the background. "Okay, got the file. Everything is ordered, and I'm sending over your invoice now."

My phone vibrates, alerting me to the incoming mail. "Okay, great. Hey, I have a parent who is covering the cost, so I will forward it to him. Please let me know if he doesn't take care of it fast enough. I'll happily pay it myself if I need to."

"Oh, who is it? I can probably tell you right away if they are going to make me wait to get paid." She laughs. "I have a list of people that I will not make so much as a sticker for until they've paid their invoice."

"I bet you do." I sigh. "People suck. I'm shocked you don't require a deposit before you order, honestly."

"Depending on who it is, I do. I'm not worried about you stiffing me, though. I know where you live."

I laugh. "True. The parent is Dustin Crenshaw. He's probably not one of your regulars."

"Nope, he's not," Avery confirms. "But, I do know him, and I'm not worried about him not paying. He's a good guy, and it's great to have him back in town. Last week, I saw him changing a tire in the rain."

"Really?"

"Yeah, Mrs. Myers was headed out of church on Sunday. The rain had just started, and she walked out of the building to find she had a flat. He was out there, soaking wet, in his church clothes, changing her tire."

"He is a good guy," I agree. "He offered to pay for the kids' shirts so they didn't have to come up with money on their own. And he volunteered to come on the Scholar's Bowl trip to chaperone the boys' hotel room."

"Whoever snatches him up next is going to be one lucky woman," she says, just as a baby in the background begins to wail loudly. "Ope, I'd better go. Duty calls."

"Bye, thanks again," I say, disconnecting the call.

I forward the email to Dustin and make myself a bowl of taco salad for dinner. By the time I slide onto a barstool and pick up my fork, I get a message from Avery saying the bill is paid.

Avery's right. Whoever ends up with Dustin Crenshaw will be one lucky lady. And is it really so wrong to hope that the lady is me?

* * *

Just like Avery had predicted, I get a text on Thursday letting me know that our shirts are done and are ready to be picked up at the bookstore. So, after work, I head that way.

Walking through the door, I find Tyler, the owner, standing behind the counter with her nose in no other than Maisie's newest book.

Of course.

She looks up and greets me with a smile. "Hey, Kristen. Welcome in. I guess you're here to pick up the shirts Avery dropped off for you."

I step towards the counter, as she slides a brown paper bag containing the shirts towards me. "I sure am, thank you."

"No problem. Hey, while you're here. Did you still need to pick up the book for the Book Club?"

I pause, blinking slowly. I remember Alex mentioning book club, but the last two weeks have been a blur, and I don't remember what she said.

Tyler holds up *Love on a Back Road* to show me.

"We're reading Maisie Bloomfield's new release. Do you need a copy of it?"

It takes everything in me not to allow my face to show exactly what I'm thinking. I shake my head. "No. I have a copy already. Thank you, though."

Tyler shrugs. "Okay, no problem at all. So, we will see you next Thursday night for our meeting. Maybe bring a snack themed to the book, or bring wine again if you want. I'm going to make Cowboy Caviar."

I nod. "Very back road sounding."

She smiles proudly. "I thought so, too. Anyway, I can't wait to hear what you thought of the book."

I pick up the bag of shirts and force a smile. "See you then! Thanks for letting me pick these up here."

She waves me off. "No problem. See you next week."

I leave the building, and I'm still shaking my head as I climb into my car. I place the bag of shirts in the passenger seat. I fire off a quick text to Dustin.

Kristen: Hey, shirts are ready. I'll send yours home with Corbin tomorrow after practice.

Dustin: Perfect. I'm excited to see how they turned out. I know Corbin is, too.

I read the text and ponder my next move for a second. It's probably not super professional to invite a parent over to my house to pick up something I can give his kid tomorrow. Still, Dustin and I haven't really been super professional so far anyway. And he has made it pretty clear that he likes me. Would it really hurt to feel things out a bit?

Kristen: If you want, you are more than welcome to swing by and pick up your shirts tonight. That is, if the anticipation is

killing you.

Dustin: I would love that. Send me your address, and I'll run by after work.

I reply with my address and then toss my phone into the passenger seat, covering my face with my hands. My heart is racing, and suddenly I have the urge to go home and redo my makeup before Dustin comes over. I don't remember the last time a guy made me feel this way, but it seems I'm in dangerous territory.

By the time I hear the sound of Dustin's truck pulling into my gravel driveway, my anxiety has calmed down a little. But that didn't stop me from running a straightener through my hair, reapplying my makeup, and brushing my teeth in anticipation of his arrival.

I can't have afternoon coffee breath or lettuce in my teeth when he arrives after all.

I stand from the couch and pause, waiting for him to come to the door. After he knocks, I count to five and then slowly make my way across the room, in an effort not to appear too eager. I swing the door open and find Dustin waiting on the other side.

He must have come straight from work. He's still wearing his work jeans with dried mud at the cuffs and on his boots.

He greets me with a wide grin. "Hey, don't you look beautiful after a day of dealing with the youth of Fawn Creek."

I can't fight the blush that I know is spreading across my face. "Thanks. Want to come in?"

Dustin frowns and glances down at his boots. "I'd love to. But, I'd have to take off my boots and my pants at this point."

I let out a loud chuckle as Jinx comes to stand at my feet.

Bending down, I scoop him into my arms.

"I usually try to at least wait until the third date to stand in a woman's living room in my underwear," he adds.

I reach over and pick a plastic bag containing his and Corbin's shirts, holding it out towards him. "I'm glad to hear you have standards at least."

He reaches forward to take the bag and pauses to scratch Jinx under his chin. Jinx leans back, reveling in the attention, and lets out a loud, appreciative purr.

"I see you're a cat whisperer," I tease. "Jinx only likes me, so you must be pretty special."

"I'd like to think I am," he answers with a grin. "Winning over your cat is half the battle."

I look back towards my bedroom door, where the other two cats are likely enjoying their thirteenth nap of the day. "Well, you have two more to work on, and they don't like anyone. Including me."

Dustin smirks. "I'm always up for a challenge."

"You're awfully cocky, Mr. Crenshaw."

He steps back and sends me a smile that makes me want to melt into a puddle in my doorway. "Not cocky. Just confident." He holds up the shirts. "Thanks for these. Corbin will be excited to see them. See you later."

"See ya." I close the front door and place Jinx on the floor before turning and resting my back against the door frame. I don't know what it is about this guy, but I'm in trouble.

And suddenly, very inspired to add to my novel.

* * *

"Now," I say, pacing the room with my arm full of folded shirts, on Friday afternoon. "If I give these to you guys today, I need you to solemnly swear you will not lose them, ruin them, or cut the sleeves off of them at least until after the season is over. Do I have your word?"

"Yes, Ms. Calhoun," the team replies in a chorus.

One by one, I pass out the shirts to everyone but Corbin, who already has his. Then the kids set up the room for practice.

"Is Corbin's dad coming today?" Heather asks, as she moves a desk into position and takes a seat.

I furrow my brows. "No, not that I'm aware of."

"Thank God," Corbin mutters under his breath.

"Man, that's too bad. He was funny." Jaxson chimes in.

"You should try living with him." Corbin retorts, not looking up from the paper in front of him, that he is doodling on. "He does not know when to stop with the dad jokes."

"Well, even so, I'm glad he's going with us on our trip." Heather shrugs. "It'll be way better than last year. Mrs. Baker's husband came with us, and he snored so loudly."

I frown. "How did his snoring bother you? Shouldn't he have been in another room?"

She nods. "He was! I could hear him through the walls! And he fell asleep everywhere. In the van, in the lobby, once at dinner. It was awful and so embarrassing. It was like my grandparents taking us to the tournament."

"And Mrs. Baker wasn't much better." Kaci chimes in. "She had a rule that lights had to be out by 8:00 pm. She wouldn't even let us be on our phones after eight. She collected them and locked them in the safe, so we weren't doing anything bad while she was sleeping. She wouldn't even let us charge them."

"Last year's tournament was almost enough to make me quit the team. But, I'm too clumsy to play basketball, and my mom is afraid I'll join a gang if I'm not on some team," Dillon informs us.

Heather blinks slowly. "Does your mom know gangs don't just take anyone? You'd probably be okay."

"Okay, that's enough," I chime in before the conversation can go any further. "Split up into two teams. We have work to do if we are going to place at State."

* * *

"Okay, team. I'll see you in class on Monday. Have a good weekend." I call out as the kids grab their backpacks and make their way out of my room at the end of practice.

As the last kid leaves, I melt into my desk chair, absolutely exhausted.

"Hey," Alex says, peeking her head into the doorway after the last kid leaves.

I see my friend and smile, welcoming the distraction. "Hey, you're here late."

She shrugs. "Noah is helping with basketball tonight, and I lost track of time working on my newest bulletin board decorations for the library. Want to grab an early dinner? I'm thinking tacos."

The thought of a meal that I don't have to eat in the silence of my own kitchen is enough to give me a second wind. I bend down and pick up my teacher's bag, sliding it over my shoulder. "Absolutely."

Within fifteen minutes, Alex and I are settled into a booth at the Mexican Restaurant in downtown Fawn Creek. There's a huge basket of chips and two bowls of salsa on the table in front of us.

I open the menu and look up at Alex with a menacing grin. "Margarita?"

She scoffs. "Absolutely not. I remember the last time you invited me here for margaritas. We had to call Noah to drive us home. I had known him for all of twenty-four hours, and that was his initial impression of me."

I laugh. "And just look at how that turned out. Monday afternoon margaritas turned into happily ever after."

Alex groans, "I can not believe he left in the middle of football practice to drive us home. I'm surprised he didn't block my number after that."

I wave her off. "Oh, I promise you, that man did not mind coming to your rescue that day. He lives to save you."

She smirks and reaches forward for a chip. "He's a good one, that's for sure."

The waiter stops to take our drink order. I close my menu and lean across the table slightly, "So, are you officially living with him yet?"

She lets out a heavy sigh. "No. I'm just staying over a lot more. I'm just trying it on for size before I commit to moving all of my stuff in."

The waiter sets our drinks down in front of us. I sip my water. "I give it Spring Break before you are fully moved in."

Alex slides her straw into her Dr. Pepper and rolls her eyes. "Anyway, that's enough wagering against me and my morals. What's up with you?"

I pause for a second, considering the question. Part of me wants to just lay it all out on the table. I could tell Alex my secret about my pen name.

I mean, it would probably do me some good to have someone to talk to. Shouldn't I have someone to share my secret with?

And if there is anyone in the world I can trust, it's Alex.

She's basically my only friend, well, besides my cats — and I can assure you they are sick and tired of listening to me yap about this.

I grew up in Fawn Creek. I've been here my whole life, but that hasn't kept me from growing up feeling like an outsider. All of the kids in my class were friends until Junior High. However, once we got to the Jr. High/High School building, we all started to discover our individual interests. And I somehow didn't fit in with any of them.

I wasn't athletic enough for sports.

I wasn't quite smart enough for the smart kids.

We didn't have a farm, so the FFA Club wasn't the place for me.

My only friends were the ones my parents didn't approve of, but they were the only ones who even made me feel welcome, so I hung out with them, against my better judgment. Suddenly, I was smoking and making terrible choices, but I felt included at least.

Of course, since then, I've grown and realized that my morals are more important than feeling accepted.

I realized I was better off on my own instead. And for years, it's been just my cats and me. Well, until Alex came along.

The waiter comes back to take our order, and when he walks away, Alex is staring at me. "What's going on with you?" she asks. "Something is definitely up."

I wave her off. "Nothing. Just a lot on my mind. Busy week at school."

Alex leans in further. "Are you sure there isn't a man involved? You seem different."

I roll my eyes. "No, there is no man. I have no use for a man other than maybe offering him up as a sacrifice."

Alex snorts. "Whatever, Kristen. You may be able to fool everyone else behind that aloof exterior, but you are not fooling me. I know deep down you are actually just an old softy."

If only Alex knew how right she actually is.

Chapter 10

Another week blows by in a blur, and it's time for the January meeting of the Fawn Creek Book Club.

Alex stops by the house to pick me up, because even though she's only known me for a few months, she knows that if she doesn't drive me, I will probably fake sick and stay home. Especially tonight.

We pull into a parking lot in front of TBR and exchange a glance as she puts her Mini Cooper in park.

"I'm excited," Alex says. "I love cute little rom-coms. This book was so good. I was sad when it ended."

"Yeah, it'll be fun." I agree, attempting to keep my voice as even and steady as possible. I know my response is dripping with sarcasm, but I can not fake excitement over this one. I mean, this has to be an author's worst nightmare, sitting in a room while people nitpick her story to death? I really should have stayed home tonight.

Alex rolls her eyes. "It's going to be great. Come on, let's go in."

Clutching the two bottles of wine I brought to share, I take a deep breath and follow Alex's lead.

We make our way into the bookstore, where we hold our book club meetings after hours. We exchange our hellos with Tyler and her friend, Madison, a local child care provider, as we place our contributions for the evening on a folding side table.

"Just the four of us again?" Alex asks as she pops the top off her container of pigs in a blanket. She pulls a bottle of mustard from her purse and sets it next to the container.

"Just the four of us," Madison confirms. "Which is fine. More cookies for us."

I eye the platter of cookies she's referring to— they appear to be sugar cookies with wildflowers delicately drawn on with frosting.

"Those are beautiful," I tell her. They look just like the flowers on the cover of the book. These are also the flowers the main male character brought to his love interest in the story.

I swallow hard.

There's just something about seeing the flowers that warms my heart. It's strange to think that I created this imaginary world, and people love it as much as I do. It's also mind-blowing that my book is not only being read for a book club, but it's also inspired cookies and menu choices.

If this is what's happening in my tiny town, what are the chances it's happening elsewhere, too?

"The flowers are a perfect match," I whisper, not meaning to say it out loud, but I do.

"Thank you," Madison grins. "Not that I made them myself. I hired it out to the bakery down the street. I hope they are as good as the book was."

"Well, I know they are going to be amazing," Alex smiles. "Every single thing I've tried from the bakery has been incredible. But, we will test them out just to be sure."

We fix our plates and settle into the emerald green chairs and couch that are arranged in a circle for our conversation.

"So," Tyler begins, with her plate balanced on her lap, "What did everyone think?"

I pick up my wine glass and take a big gulp. *Here goes nothing.*

I can already feel my confidence going out the window.

"I loved it," Alex gushes. "The characters had so much depth, and every one of them developed beautifully. I think every woman wants a Chad in her life."

Madison scrunches her nose. "That's the only part I didn't like. The story was great, but who names a main male character Chad? A Chad isn't a hero, he's a guy that punches holes in walls and chugs energy drinks."

Tyler laughs and shakes her head. "No, that's Kyle, not Chad."

"She's right," Alex chimes in, waving her pig in a blanket in the air. "Chad is a frat boy, and Kyle slams energy drinks and punches holes in walls."

I slam the rest of my wine. I knew it was going to be hard listening to people criticize my work, but the names of my characters? Really? This is the complex I'm going to develop now?

"Okay, okay. I think we can all agree that we don't love the name Chad, but what about the story? I really enjoyed it." Tyler chimes in, interrupting the argument. "I can see why Maisie Bloomfield is having a moment right now. Honestly, I've been working my way through her entire catalog here lately, and I can see why. She's an amazing storyteller."

I blush and almost thank Tyler for the compliment. OMG, I need to lay off the wine. I'm going to out myself.

"I agree," chimes in Alex. "Her stories are fun and funny. They are lighthearted and just the thing the world needs right now, while everything else feels really hard. She has a fan in me for sure."

"Me too," Madison agrees. "I think she will become one of those automatic buy authors for me, you know, the ones that put out a book and you instantly buy it, not even knowing what it's about?"

"I have a few of those myself," Tyler says before turning towards me. "Kristen, what did you think?"

I quickly finish chewing my food and swallow loudly. "Um, yeah. I liked it."

Of course, I liked it. I wrote it. Not that I can admit that to anyone else.

Madison shrugs. "You can be honest with us, it's okay. I know this probably isn't your normal kind of read. You look like the psychological thriller type."

Tyler shakes her head and holds a hand up. "Oh no, Kristen told me she already owned the book when I asked her about it last week. I think someone here might have a dirty little secret."

Tyler's words cause my heart to race, and I nearly choke on the piece of cookie in my mouth. Could she know? Could everyone know? How would they know?

"Wh..." I stutter. "What's that?"

She grins, "That you're a secret rom-com lover, of course."

I let out a sigh of relief over the fact that I have not been busted. "Oh. Well, actually, I do like to read rom-coms. I enjoy them, and it's not so much a secret. I don't advertise it to the world."

"She has to keep up her tough exterior," Alex smirks. "She likes to make these sarcastic, dry comments and keep everyone guessing all the time, but deep down I think she is actually a hopeless romantic."

Once again, I keep my voice steady and dry. "Yep, Alex, you have me all figured out."

Alex throws her head back into a laugh. "See? You definitely sound like you are joking, but I don't think you are. I think underneath the tough exterior, you are just a girly girl."

I look around at Tyler and Madison, who are both smirking at me. I roll my eyes. "Hey. When did this discussion become about me instead of about Maisie Bloomfield? You guys need to get back on track."

Madison sighs loudly. "Fine. Can we talk about the make-out scene, then? The one in the bed of his truck in the hay field? For a closed-door book, it was almost spicy."

"Gah, it was so good." Tyler groans.

Madison nods. "Yeah, it was. Made me totally forgive the guy for his name."

"Not this again," Tyler laughs as she steps towards the cookies. She picks one up and turns back to face us. "But, agreed. This book hit all the marks for me. Five-star read."

"She might actually be my new favorite author," Alex admits. "The girls at school are even reading one of her books in book club. They love her, too." She pauses for a second. "Tyler, you know what would be cool? If you could get her to come to the store and do a signing."

This time, I actually *do* choke on my cookie.

"Holy crap," Madison springs from her seat as though she's ready to give me the Heimlich maneuver. "Are you okay?"

I nod, clearing the cookie. Tyler refills my wine glass, and I take a drink to wash it down. "Sorry about that."

"Glad you're okay," Tyler sighs before turning back to Alex. "Actually, I looked her up. She's like a ghost—no social media accounts. No website. Her author bio on Amazon is even pretty bare. It's like she doesn't want to be found."

Alex frowns. "That's a bummer. An appearance from someone like Maisie would bring in quite a crowd to the store."

Tyler shrugs. "Hey, if you can track her down, I'd be happy to host."

I swallow another mouthful of wine and look up at the clock. This is going to be a long night. My heart is pounding in my ears.

"Why do you think she's so hidden?" Madison asks and then ponders the question. "Maybe she's just an old lady who can't figure out how to do social media or build a website."

Tyler shrugs. "Maybe, but you'd still think she would have an email address at least.

Alex picks at the icing on her cookie. "What if she's a man? Not just any man. Like a sweaty, hairy man that lives in his mom's basement?"

Tyler rolls her eyes. "I think the old lady theory is much closer."

"What do you think, Kristen?" Madison asks.

I shrug. "I don't know. Maybe she is just someone who wants to keep her private life private."

"Oh, maybe she's famous," Madison says excitedly. "Like a celebrity or a singer or a politician."

Alex shrugs. "She could be literally anyone. Maybe we will never know."

That's the plan, Alex. That's the plan.

After book club, I walk into the house and kick off my shoes at the door, pausing to take in the quiet. Jinx, of course, is already at my feet, waiting to be picked up, while Ash and Tripp don't so much as bat an eye at me. I scoop up Jinx, give him a scratch under the chin, and then place him down on his bed before moving to the kitchen for a glass of water. I need it after half a bottle of wine I drank tonight.

The meeting went better than I expected, thank goodness. There was something strange yet endearing about listening to them gush over how much they love Maisie and, in turn, enjoy my stories. Of course, there was the whole Chad debacle. Not all Chads are frat guys, just like not all Kyle's punch holes s in drywall, and not all Karen's are insufferable and demanding to speak to your manager. Nonetheless, it's something to keep in mind while naming my next set of characters, I suppose.

Leaning against the counter, I pull my notebook from my bag, looking over notes I've scribbled for my next scenes, but my mind keeps wandering to Dustin. It's no secret that my male character looks, acts, and sounds like him. And that's no surprise because he's been heavy on my mind. But maybe that's just the romance author in me. I'm just looking for romance in any situation and dreaming up couples that don't belong together. Right?

I glance at the calendar hanging next to the fridge. The weekend with the words Scholar's Bowl Trip that I scrawled in red ink is looming closer. How am I going to be with him all weekend, knowing that I've been spending all my spare time turning him into a book character? Now I understand the fascination with book boyfriends, and I think I may have created my best one yet.

* * *

"Do you guys need anything else?" I ask, leaning across the table to refill a coffee cup in front of David Richardson. I've known Mr. Richardson most of my life, as he was a fourth-grade teacher when I was in school. It's Saturday morning, and I'm once again covering a shift at the diner.

"No, dear, we're fine," his wife replies with a soft smile. She picks up the ceramic mug and lifts it to her hot pink lipstick-covered lips. "Are you still teaching at the school?"

"Oh yes. High School English." I tell her. "I imagine I'll be there for as long as they will have me."

She smiles softly. "I bet those kids love you. Back when I was in school, all we had were a bunch of mean old ladies for teachers. No one liked going to school."

I smirk, shifting my weight as I stand with the coffee pot in one hand. "Well, I'm probably not too far from becoming a mean old lady myself. I remember when I was in school, I thought my teachers were old. And I'm the same age now as they were then."

Mr. Richardson lets out a chuckle, not looking up from his newspaper. "Well, as long as you don't become mean, you'll probably be okay."

"I'm a little mean." I shrug.

"She doesn't have a mean bone in her body," a man's voice chimes in to join our conversation.

I raise a brow and turn to look at the source of the sound. It's Dustin.

I excuse myself from the Richardsons' and spin on my heel to return to the coffee pot to the machine behind the counter before responding. "I'm a little bit mean," I assure him. "You haven't seen me play Uno."

Dustin chuckles and takes a seat at the counter. "Sounds like a date. I'll pick up a deck of Uno cards this afternoon."

I smile on just one side of my face. "Oh, really? You think you could handle that?"

He shrugs. "I mean, it's not what I would have envisioned for our first date, but whatever it takes to get you to go out with me."

The bell in the kitchen window dings, and Dad calls out, "Order up!"

I retrieve the Styrofoam food containers he left with an order slip. Dustin's name is scrawled across the bottom. I place the boxes in a plastic bag and set it on the counter between us. "Need any silverware?"

He shakes his head. "Nope. I'm taking it home. Corbin's starving, and I haven't had time to make it to the store yet. All my parents keep on hand is unflavored oatmeal."

I tie the bag closed and slide it across the counter to him. "I can't believe a man who still lives with his parents thinks he's going to take me on a date." I tease, before sliding his ticket towards him. "$26.37 is your total."

He pulls his wallet from his back pocket and flips it open, then removes two twenties and hands them to me. "Keep the change."

I roll my eyes. "You don't have to do that, you know."

"What?"

I punch the amount into the register. "Leave me a thirteen-dollar tip just for handing your food to you. I was joking about not going on a date with you."

I place the change on the counter between us. He slides it back towards me. "That wasn't my plan, but it's nice to know that you're at least willing to go out with me. What are you doing tonight?"

I frown. "I'm covering the closing shift. Tomorrow night?"

He shakes his head. "Family dinner. I mean, you are more than welcome to come, but I'd like to try at least to get you to fall in love with me before my parents embarrass me in front of you."

I shake my head. "Damn. I was really looking forward to seeing pictures of you in a bathtub on our first date."

Dustin lowers his voice and leans in closer. "If you want to see me naked, all you have to do is ask."

I swallow hard. "That's not..."

Dustin picks up the bag and slides off the stool. "Well, I'd better get these pancakes back to the kid. Well, eventually, we will figure out a time that I can take you out on a proper date. If that's okay with you. "

"Yes," I agree. "I'd like that."

"I'll shoot you a message later," he promises. "Have a good day."

Dustin picks up the bag, and I watch as he makes her way out the front door. I pick up the tip that he left sitting on the counter and slide it into my apron pocket just as my mother steps behind me and clears her throat.

"He's cute," she says with a wide smile as I turn to face her.

I busy myself with wiping an imaginary spot on the counter. "Is he? I hadn't noticed."

She lets out a deep laugh. "Oh, I saw you not noticing as you watched him walk out the door. Are you going to go on a date with him?"

I shrug. "Maybe."

"You should. I hope you do."

"We'll see," I say, thanking my lucky stars at the bell above the door jingles, and a family of four walks in. I pick up a stack of menus and make my way towards them, escaping the conversation with my mom.

I have had a hard-and-fast rule for years: I tell my mother

nothing about my dating life until it gets serious. In fact, I've often fantasized about calling my parents on my wedding day and asking them to close the diner and run down to the church for a surprise. When they arrive, I'll be standing at the end of the aisle. The only people in attendance —myself, the groom, and the preacher— will yell surprise, and then we will be hitched before the lunch rush begins.

However, I never expected my dating life and my personal life to collide quite this much. Accepting a date with Dustin violates my rule against dating someone from Fawn Creek. I can only imagine how many more of my rules I'll be breaking because of this guy.

Chapter 11

Before I know it, the weekend is over, and I'm back to school with a draft that is 50% done and no chance of writing this week in sight. Monday and Tuesday, I stay busy with teaching by day and waiting tables by night. The girl who usually waits tables in the evening is down with the flu, and being the amazing, perfect daughter that I am, I agree to cover her shifts for a few days.

My perfect daughter streak comes to an end on Wednesday; instead, I have to sit at the school for nearly a twelve-hour day due to parent-teacher conferences.

Conferences are high on my list of things that I do not enjoy about teaching. It's a short list, but it exists. To be clear, the hatred has nothing to do with the conferences themselves. The parents who come are great. Those parents ask questions and show a general interest in what their kids are learning.

However, those parents are few and far between. In fact, those parents aren't really the ones who need to come because they already have established relationships with the school and keep tabs on their kids, their grades, and any missing assignments.

The ones that I would actually like to see, the parents of the slackers and the troublemakers, rarely show their faces. I suppose I don't blame them; if their kids are this much of a pain in the butt for me, I can only imagine what they put mom and dad through.

Conferences are set to start at 4:00 sharp, and the building doors are locked for an hour after school gets out. This allows the teachers to eat dinner and take a short break before conferences start. However, for some reason, everyone seems to want to use this hour to stand around and chat in the teachers' lounge. That is certainly not my idea of a break, but I surely won't be missing out on a free catered meal either. I will not be hanging out in here, just getting my food and getting out.

I make my way into the lounge and poke my head inside. Just as I expected, the room is packed with teachers who look just as exhausted as I am, filling their plates with street tacos, Mexican rice, and chips with salsa. At least if they are going to make us work late, they are feeding us well. I join the line behind Alex and Noah.

The combination of the room packed with people and the warming trays for the food is making it uncomfortably warm.

Alex turns to greet me with a smile. Noah is standing with his back to her while talking to Chris, the Biology teacher. "Hey! Fancy meeting you here."

"Hey," I pick up a plate and fan myself with it. "What are you doing here? The school librarian usually doesn't come to these things."

Alex shrugs. "I don't know. I figure this is a great chance to open up the library and show all of the parents the progress I've made. Or maybe they'll feel bad and buy a few books off my wish list."

I smirk as we step forward in line. "If any parents bother to come see me, I'll be sure to send them your way."

This causes Alex to frown. "Do parents not usually come? I thought that was the whole point."

I shake my head. "Some do. But not all or even a lot. Lord knows they won't ever miss a basketball game, but their child's academic progress isn't worth getting out of the house for. Maybe we should do conferences during games to save everyone time."

I ponder my suggestion for a second. "Actually, maybe I'll suggest that to Gerald for next year. It could be like speed dating during halftime. They could put folding tables on the court and make a spectacle out of it."

Alex blinks slowly. "You might be on to something."

I step towards the door, carrying my plate. "They'd better not ever let me become an administrator. Life would become really ridiculous around here real quick."

* * *

Once back in my room, I lose track of time, eating my dinner and grading papers so that I won't have to take anything home this weekend.

I'm just entering my final grade when there's a knock at my classroom door. I check the time on my phone screen—four o'clock. The first, overachieving parent, is right on time.

Naturally, it's Kaci's mom, Sabrina.

I close my laptop and welcome her into the room. She takes a seat in one of the chairs I have positioned in front of my desk.

"Hi, how are you?" she asks, her voice chipper as though she is trying to match her bright pink sweater and permed blonde hair perfectly. Sabrina and I have met before, on many occasions. All through Kaci's high school career, she has never missed a conference. In fact, she never misses anything.

Sabrina is always the first parent to volunteer to help with dances, fundraisers, and mock interviews. Truly, she is one of the most involved parents in the entire school. She will be truly missed next year when Kaci graduates.

"I'm great," I reply. "How are you? How is senior year?"

She frowns dramatically. "It's a lot," she admits. "Kaci is my baby, and knowing that she is going to graduate in a few months is a lot harder than I expected. I've already gotten three other kids through high school; this shouldn't be new, but for some reason it is. It's so different when you are launching your last baby into the world."

"I'm sorry, but if it helps any, you've obviously done a great job with her. She's a good kid, and her grades are phenomenal."

"That's always nice to hear," she admits. "I'm pretty proud of that kid."

"You should be. She is doing great in my class. She has a 102% right now; that kid never skips a chance for extra credit. And she's doing awesome in Scholar's Bowl. She has really stepped up and taken the team captain position very seriously."

Sabrina beams. "She loves Scholar's Bowl, and she has just gone on and on about how much she loves having you as the coach."

The compliment causes me to blush just a little. "I'm enjoying it. Speaking of, I have a permission slip for you to sign for the trip to Manhattan. I'm surprised you're not coming along." I slide the note across the desk towards her.

Sabrina scans over the slip and signs it before sliding it back to me. "I would, but my husband said no," she laughs. "He and I already had a trip planned for that weekend. I was going to reschedule, but he is adamant that it's time for me to step back and let her start doing things without me."

I shrug. "Well, I guess she will be eighteen soon, so he might be on to something. Besides, I'm sure you two could use a break."

Sabrina nods dramatically. "Oh yes, we do. You have no idea."

"Well, don't worry about this trip at all. She will be fine, and we will have a great time. There are two girls and four boys on the team. And honestly, I couldn't ask for a better group. Things shouldn't get too wild at all."

"I'm sure you're right. I can't wait to hear all about it. I plan to pack the kids some snack bags for the trip and drop them off the day before. Let me know if anyone has any allergies."

"That would be amazing. I'll check with the kids tomorrow during practice and get back to you as soon as I can." I say, glancing up at the clock. "That's all I have for you, unless you have something else?"

Sabrina shakes her head. "Nope. I'm good. I guess that's it. My very last conference."

"And you ended on a great note," I say, standing from my desk. "Thanks for coming by."

Sabrina takes my cue and stands from her seat. "Well, thank you, Ms. Calhoun. Please let me know if you think of anything you need for the trip, or if you need anything else at all. I am happy to help wherever it is needed."

We exchange our good-byes, and she makes her way out the door, while I settle in for my next parent to arrive. If only every conference could be as quick and painless as that one.

While there is no set schedule, I can pretty much guess every parent who will come in tonight. I have a few parents, like

Sabrina, who would never miss a chance to visit about their child. Then, I reached out to several parents and asked them to make time to come. But who knows if they will even bother to show up.

After Sabrina, I have a series of parents come through my doors. Some walk in quietly, bracing themselves for the worst, some walk in with heads high, already having checked their child's grades long before tonight... and yet a few walk in seeming to be surprised even to find out that their child is indeed taking an English class. And as usual, there were plenty that never showed up at all.

One dad even walked in to announce, "I'm just here because the coach said I needed to be."

I wasn't sure whether I was more surprised that Noah told a grown man he had to come to conferences, or that the man listened. But, nonetheless. I take the time to print a list of his son's 14 missing assignments, likely in his locker, under a pile of dirty gym clothes and forgotten Stanley cups.

It's safe to say that Billy is probably grounded.

By the time the end of the evening is approaching, I'm well past exhausted. I glance at the clock. It's been a solid thirty minutes since the last parent stepped through my door, but I have to be here until seven regardless. I've caught up on grading every assignment, cleaned out my desk, and made a few notes about what will happen next in *Lessons In Love.*

I'm itching to get out of the building and get into my little pink office and get to writing. In fact, maybe it wouldn't hurt things if I just got out my laptop and worked just a little. I'm sure no one else will be by tonight anyway.

Against my better judgment, I open my laptop and click around on the screen, opening the document just as I'm interrupted by a gentle knock on the door.

Quickly, I close the computer and look up, surely looking like a child that's been caught doing something they were told not to. However, I'm shocked to find Dustin standing in the doorway, clutching a brown paper bag in his hand.

This isn't the man I'm used to— the man I've interacted with shows up in dirty work boots and jeans with a dingy baseball cap.

Tonight, he's different. He put a genuine effort into his appearance, and it shows.

He's freshly showered. I can tell because I can smell his body wash as he takes a seat across from me. It's woodsy and clean and makes me want to inch closer to him.

He's still wearing jeans, but these jeans have never seen a day of work. They are clean, pressed, and possibly starched. He's wearing a plaid pearl-snap button-down shirt with a white undershirt peeking out at the top. He's wearing a baseball cap, but this one is clean, too. It's stark white and has likely never been worn before.

"Hi," I say, swallowing hard, hoping he can't tell that I'm checking out every inch of him.

"Hi," he replies, opening the bag and pulling out a small tin. "I stopped at the bakery today, and I got myself a cheesecake. And I just thought you might like one, too. After being at work all day and stuck here late."

He slides a small disposable tin of cheesecake with a chocolate swirled top towards me. I peer down to look at my treat. "Thank you."

Dustin frowns. "Is this weird? I should have asked first," he shakes his head. "What if you don't like cheesecake? Or chocolate. What if you're lactose intolerant?"

I let out a hearty laugh. "Well, I love cheesecake and chocolate, and I tolerate dairy very well. Thank you. This is very thoughtful, and I will enjoy it for sure when I get home tonight."

Dustin smirks. "I'm not very good at this, if you can't tell."

"Parent-teacher conferences?"

He sighs. "Flirting. Or trying to flirt with a beautiful woman."

My heart flutters at his omission. *That's definitely going to be a line in the book.*

He continues. "I know I am good at pretending to be cocky, but I'm actually not really very good at this dating thing. In fact, I haven't even tried since Karina passed away. She and I were together for fourteen years, and trying to start over is a lot to take in."

"You're doing better than you think," I say just above a whisper.

Dustin and I sit in silence for at least a full minute before I finally remember that I'm the teacher and he's the parent, and we are here for a reason.

I take a deep breath and turn towards my computer. "Corbin is doing great," I say, trying to keep my voice steady, as I open my grade book software. "He has a 96% in my class."

"Great," Dustin repeats.

The silence in the room is deafening. I stand from my seat and walk across the room.

I pull Corbin's journal from the shelf and carry it back to Dustin, handing it to him.

"One thing I have the kids do in every class period is I have them write a journal entry. I put a prompt on the whiteboard, and they take five minutes to write."

Dustin smirks. "I remember he used to do this in preschool back home. His mom kept all of his old journals on the bookshelf in the living room. She loved to look back over them from time to time."

"Well, this will be sent home at the end of the year. I tell the kids to give them to their parents, but I can't guarantee most make it that far."

Dustin opens the book's cover and flips through the pages. "What I did over Christmas break. My dad dragged me against my will to live in a new town so we could be closer to my grandparents," he reads and then lets out a loud groan. "I hope one day he forgives me for uprooting him."

Without thinking, I reach across the table and squeeze his hand. "He will."

Dustin looks at my hand, and I pull it back quickly.

"I'm sorry." I apologize. "That was unprofessional."

"I'm not going to report you."

"Oh, thank you for that," I reply with a chuckle as he slides the journal back to me. I carry it back to the shelf and turn to face him. "I don't have any concerns about Corbin. He's a great kid. He's adjusting well and making friends. He's smart and funny and a great artist, and I'm very happy to have him on the Scholar's Bowl team."

Dustin lets out a sigh of relief. "You have no idea how good it feels to hear that. I've been worried that I screwed up bringing him here."

I wave Dustin off as I work to pack my tote bag. "Kids are resilient, and Fawn Creek is a great place to grow up. He will do just fine here. He already is."

"Good." Dustin stands from his seat and stretches. "Are you done here for the night?"

"Yes, thankfully. It's been a long day."

"I'll walk you out," he offers.

Before I can respond, I find myself grabbing my things and leading him through the classroom door. I lock it behind me, and then we make our way down the hall in a comfortable silence. It's ten minutes past seven now, and the halls are empty. It seems not a single teacher wasted a second to get out of here for the night. The whole school is a ghost town.

He holds the heavy glass door open for me, and we step outside into the cool winter air. I look towards my car and point towards it in the parking lot. "That's me."

"I'm right down the row from you," he says, pointing to his red extended cab pickup truck. "I'll walk you the rest of the way."

As we approach my car, I walk around to the passenger side and place my bag in the seat before turning back towards him. "Thanks for walking me out."

He smirks. "Of course. Have to keep you safe on the mean streets of Fawn Creek. What are you doing after this?"

I shrug. "Going home and eating cheesecake, I suppose. Why?"

He shrugs. "Just wondering what a beautiful teacher does when she goes home at the end of the day."

I look out over the empty parking lot and back to him as I lean slightly against my car. "Oh, you know, normal teacher stuff. Grading papers and swimming in my piles of money I make from teaching."

Dustin lets out an appreciative laugh, but when he stops, his gaze falls on my lips.

"What are you thinking?" I ask.

"I'm thinking I really want to kiss you right now. What are

you thinking?"

"That I think you should kiss me right now," I whisper in response.

With that, Dustin takes one more step towards me. He wraps an arm around my waist and pulls me in close. Our bodies press together, and suddenly, the rest of the world no longer exists. The sound of the nearby highway disappears, and the thought of being seen by an onlooker doesn't even cross my mind. It's just the two of us.

I look up at him, and he leans down, crashing his mouth into mine. I lift my hands to find his back, pulling him in closer to me, as if it's even possible at this point, after what somehow feels like too long and also not long enough, Dustin pulls back.

"That was..." he whispers. "Wow."

"Yeah, it was," I agree with a heavy sigh. I look at the car, then back at him. "I'd better go."

"Probably," he laughs. He takes a step back, freeing me from where I was pressed between him and the car.

Holding my hand, Dustin leads me to the driver's side door and opens it for me.

Still unsure what to do or say, I climb in and look back up at him. Without a word, he leans down and quickly kisses me once again. This time it's softer and gentler, almost as though this is something we do every day.

We exchange our goodbyes, and I back out of my parking spot, still reeling from what just took place.

My heart is racing, my stomach is full of butterflies, and everything in me wants to turn around. But, I don't.

Instead, I drive home and try to make sense of what just happened. And for the first time in a long time, I've found someone who makes me want to feel this way over and over again.

Chapter 12

I roll out of bed at 6:00 on Tuesday morning to get ready for work, and I'm met with a text on my phone. It's from Dustin.

Dustin: Hi. I hope I didn't overstep last night.

Reading his words reawakens the butterflies in my stomach that fluttered relentlessly until I fell asleep last night.

Kristen: Definitely not an overstep.

Dustin: Thank God. Otherwise, next weekend would have been really awkward.

Kristen: It would have been a very interesting Scholar's Bowl trip, that's for sure. But, no, you are more than good.

Dustin: Good enough for you to agree to go on a date with me this weekend?

I read the text and pause before answering his question. Yes, of course, especially after that kiss last night, I am very interested in going on a date with him.

In fact, I am interested in much more than a date if we are being completely honest.

However, I do have other people to consider as well.

Not administration. They don't really care if you date a parent as long as you keep it off school property. Which, of course, I already messed that one up last night. Oops.

I definitely need to make sure we leave the school before our next makeout session. But I do want to make sure this doesn't make anything weird for Corbin.

If nothing else, Dustin and I need to give him a heads-up before going out in public together. Word will spread fast, and it would be unfair for Corbin to be the last to know.

I fire off another text to Dustin.

Kristen: What about Corbin?

Dustin: Well, I don't generally take my kid on dates. And I have to say, he is getting pretty good at staying home alone for a few hours. I even let him use the microwave now.

I let out a loud sigh.

Kristen: I mean... does Corbin know about us?

Dustin: About how good it felt to kiss you last night, finally? Or how I would have liked to carry that on for hours? No, I haven't told him. Should I? I'm new to this dating my kids' teacher thing.

I let out another groan before I respond.

Kristen: Well, I'm not saying the kid needs details. But I am saying that you should at least give him a heads-up before we go on a date. I know you've been away from Fawn Creek for a little while, but the gossip mill in this town is still going strong. I want to make sure he hears it from you before he hears it from someone else. I don't want to catch him off guard.

Dustin: Deal. I will tell him tonight that we are going on a date this weekend.

* * *

I make my way into work and get through the morning without any incidents.

Before I know it, my fifth-hour freshman kids are stepping into the classroom.

Not that I would ever admit it to the kids, but this is my favorite grade level. They are like baby high schoolers.

They are still young enough not to think they know everything, and they even humor me by laughing at my jokes from time to time. Unlike the upper-level students, who have been tired of listening to me make the same out-of-pocket comments year after year.

Nash and Corbin make their way into the room just before the bell rings, taking their seats near the back of the room.

"Okay, guys. You know the drill," I tell the class, looking out at them from my desk. "Get your journals, and today's writing prompt is on the board."

"When I grow up, I want to be..." Nash reads the topic out

loud to the rest of the class.

"A dinosaur," answers Drake, a brown-haired boy with a mullet, under his breath.

"Make sure to tell me what kind of dinosaur, Drake," I reply, not looking up from my desk. "Be really descriptive."

"Hey, Ms. C. Speaking of descriptive," another boy, Dawson, chimes in. "When were you going to tell us about your new boyfriend?"

Dawson's question makes my jaw drop and my heart race.

This can not be happening right now.

"I don't have a new boyfriend," I answer quickly. "And this is not the time or the place to be talking about my personal life."

"Well, for not having a boyfriend, you were sure invested in kissing some dude last night in the school parking lot," Dawson chimes in. "Was that Corbin's dad? It looked like him."

Dammit.

I jump to my feet. "Dawson hallway, now," I say sternly, pointing towards the door.

Dawson stands from his seat and shrugs, making his way to the hall.

I close the door behind me and turn to face him with my arms crossed over my chest. "Dude. I asked you to stop."

"I was just kidding," he responds.

"No. You weren't. You were trying to make both me and Corbin uncomfortable. None of that is your business, and definitely none of it is the business of the entire classroom." I shake my head. "I ought to send you to the Principal's office."

Dawson's smile fades. "Oh, please don't. If I get sent to the office again, my mom is going to shut off my phone. She told me last week."

"Well, maybe you don't need a phone."

"Bro. Please. Do you know how many Snap streaks would be ruined if I get grounded?" His lip quivers. I think this kid might actually start crying. Glad to know I've still got it.

I let out a heavy sigh. "Fine. But when an adult says quit, that means quit. Don't keep egging it on."

Dawson holds up both hands. "I'm sorry. It won't happen again."

I place my hand on the doorknob to step back into the classroom as he speaks up again, "But really. Are you and Corbin's dad a thing?"

"Back to class," I say sternly, trying to steady my voice.

I make my way back into the classroom and instruct the kids to finish their journal entries and work on the assignment on the board. Then, I pick up my phone and fire a text explaining to Dustin what just happened.

After that message is sent, I send a message to Gerald, informing him that I am in a relationship with a parent.

I would have told him, of course. It's the proper thing to do. But, I would have liked to have waited until Dustin and I went on an actual date. What's the point in getting anyone else involved before the two of us go out for a meal? We might not even like each other that much. It might end up being an entire flop. But now, I know that half of the town will be whispering about us before we even sit down for a meal.

So much for keeping my private life private.

* * *

"So, wait. What happened?" Dustin asks.

It's just after 3:00. All the kids have left for the day, and I'm in my classroom with my phone pressed to my ear, trying to explain this mess to Dustin before he talks to Corbin.

"We got caught, which of course we did. We were making out in the school parking lot after all." I groan. "And a kid announced it in class right in front of Corbin."

Dustin snickers. "I don't know that I would consider that a makeout session."

"Well, what would you call it then?"

"A kiss."

I scoff. "That was not just a kiss."

I've *never* experienced a kiss that made me feel like that before.

"Then what was it?"

"I told you. A makeout session."

"Kristen. I need to come over and show you the difference between a makeout session and a kiss." Dustin laughs. "There is a huge difference."

The thought of him being in my house, where we could be all alone, causes my heart to race.

I swallow hard, trying to fight that feeling. It's not working.

"Anyway, I'm not trying to argue semantics with you. I'm just saying that Corbin knows. Hell, the entire town probably knows at this point. The kid who announced it has quite a big mouth, and from personal experience, I know he got that from his mother. It's probably going to be in the newspaper this week."

Dustin pauses for a beat. "Well, it's not ideal. Definitely not the way I wanted to tell him, but at least he knows, I guess."

"I'm really sorry."

"I'm not." Dustin laughs. "It took a lot of guts to kiss you, and I'm just glad you didn't punch me. I'll talk to Corbin. Are you going to be in trouble at school?"

I shake my head as though he can see me. "I don't know. I sent an email to my boss, but he hasn't responded. He might be writing up my pink slip as we speak."

"I highly doubt that."

Just then, we are interrupted by a knock on the door. I look up and see Gerald looking at me through the window. I hold up a finger to say one minute before turning my attention back to Dustin.

"I gotta go. My consequences are knocking at the door."

We exchange our good-byes, and I end the call before taking a deep breath and moving to open the door for my boss.

"Hi," I greet Gerald, swinging the door open towards him. "Come on in. I assume you got my email."

The man nods, his face is unreadable, and for half a second, I wonder if I'm going to suddenly become a full-time waitress working for my parents.

"I did," he confirms. "And I want you to know that I talked to Dawson as well."

I nod. This is it. My fate is sealed, all because I finally kissed a man who was worth kissing.

Gerald continues. "I informed him that teachers and staff are allowed to have personal lives, and the next time he finds it appropriate to bring up any information about a staff member in a classroom full of his peers, he will be serving a month's worth of Saturday school."

I blink slowly. "We don't even have Saturday school."

Gerald shrugs. "Dawson didn't know that."

I let out a low chuckle. "So, I'm not in trouble?"

Gerald laughs so fiercely that it causes his belly to shake. "No, of course not. While I would prefer that you keep your...

um... private interactions more private, I know that these things happen." Gerald shrugs. "Now, if you had been doing more than you were or if it were during school hours or in the building, it might be a different story."

I nod. "Of course, you do not have to worry about any of that," I assure him. "And the parking lot scene will not happen again either."

"I'm sure it won't," he says, making his way towards the door. "Well, I'd better head home for the day, and I'm sure you want to do the same. Have a good night, Kristen."

"Good night," I reply as I watch him leave the room, finally letting out a sigh of relief.

I fire off a text to Dustin to let him know I still have a job for the time being, then pack up my things and head home for the day.

Just as I'm about to walk out the door, my phone vibrates in my pocket.

Dustin: I'll talk to Corbin when he gets home. But I haven't gotten an angry text from him yet, so that's a good sign.

Before I can answer, another text comes through.

Dustin: So, about that date... Friday night? Dinner? Maybe we can revisit that kiss vs makeout session discussion.

I read over his text and immediately feel my face grow warm as I blush. I can't remember the last time a man made me feel like this, but my goodness, I don't want it to end.

Chapter 13

"Okay, guys. Great work today," I say to the team as I look down to check my watch. "Go ahead and pack everything up. Don't forget, next Friday there's no meeting because we will be on our way to Manhattan."

"I'm so excited!" Heather says, clapping her hands together. "I've already started packing."

I furrow my brows. "Heather, don't forget we are only staying for one night. You don't have to bring half of your life with you."

Heather winces. Apparently, I'm too late with that warning.

"Also, I only have a permission slip for Kaci since her mom attended conferences last night." I scan the room, making eye contact with each child to ensure they are paying attention. "Permission slips for everyone else are on my desk. Please make sure you pick one up on your way out the door today and bring it back on Monday. If I don't have your permission slip by the end of the day on Tuesday, you can't go. And that's not my rule, that's the schools."

"Yes, ma'am," the kids reply in unison.

I work on packing up my teacher bag for the night, as the team puts the supplies in my closet and begins to file out of the room.

"Do you need a slip from me?" Corbin asks as he approaches my desk carefully. He and I haven't spoken much since the incident on Tuesday. Dustin told me he spoke to him, and Corbin did not seem to be bothered by the two of us dating. But that hasn't kept me from treading very carefully anyway. Relationships with teens can be very sensitive, and I don't want to make high school any harder than it already is.

"No," I answer. "Since your dad is coming with us, you won't need one," I assure him.

Corbin nods. "Okay," he answers, but he doesn't move from where he stands.

"Anything else?" I ask, resting my hands in a folded position on the desk.

Corbin shakes his head. "No, I guess not," he answers, but he still doesn't step away. "Are you going on a date with my dad tonight?"

The question catches me off guard. "Um. Yes. I am. Is that okay?"

He nods. "Yeah. It's cool."

I check around the room, ensuring the rest of the team has left before looking back up at him. "Corbin," I begin, keeping my voice as steady as possible. "I promise I'm going to try to keep this as normal as possible for you. I do like your dad, but I promise I'm not going to start hanging out at your house right off the bat or calling you out in class or anything else. This is a new thing for me, too. We are in this together, okay?"

"Okay," he nods. He sits in my words for a second before speaking again. "I guess I'll see you later, Ms. Calhoun."

I smile softly. "See you Monday, Corbin."

I pause and watch him leave before melting back into my chair, finally allowing myself to breathe normally.

I hope this man is worth all the emotion this relationship is causing me.

I leave the school and drive home, buzzing with excitement for the evening ahead of me. I have to admit, getting the "it's cool" from Corbin feels like a tiny win. I never want to make one of my students uncomfortable, and to be honest, I've never even considered dating a parent before.

Truthfully, I haven't given much attention to dating in a long time. Sure, there have been dinners here and there, but truly, I could have told you before even walking out the door to see those men that those dates were headed nowhere fast.

I've also had a strict rule that I would not date anyone from Fawn Creek. Not only is Fawn Creek a tiny town, but I basically have felt like the dating pool is quite shallow. Also, dating out of town helps ensure my private life is kept private.

But Dustin is different.

In fact, Dustin is the first man in a long time that I have really wanted to create a future with. And I want to make sure this goes right.

I make my way into the house, pausing for a second to scratch Jinx under his chin. Per usual, Ash and Trip don't bother moving from their beds. They couldn't possibly have afternoon naps interrupted.

I shower and wash my hair, not that my job is a dirty one, but something is soothing about washing away the day when I leave the school.

With my hair wrapped in a towel and another towel around my body, I walk into my room, staring at my closet.

Suddenly, I have no idea what a thirty-year-old teacher wears on a date with the father of one of her students. This is not something I learned in college, that's for sure.

I stare at my row of black sweaters, blazers, and professional pants for another few minutes before deciding to call in reinforcements.

"Hey," Alex answers the phone in a chipper tone. "What's up?"

"I need help. Can you come over?"

"Be there in five."

While waiting for Alex, I put on a lounge set, so I'm not answering the door in a towel, and then I make sure the door to my office is locked. The last thing I need is for her to walk in there accidentally. I'm preparing for a date, and it's all the drama I need for one weekend.

I'm in the middle of blow-drying my hair when Alex walks into my room.

While I'm finishing, she helps herself to my closet. But when I turn off the dryer, Alex is looking at me with a very disappointed look on her face.

"Please tell me you have more clothes than this," she frowns. "Maybe in your guest room?" She motions towards the bedroom next door, my office.

I shake my head, probably a bit too rapidly. The thought of her even attempting to check that room causes my heart to race. "Nope, that's it."

"Kristen," now she sounds like she is scolding me. "Literally all you own are work clothes and lounge sets. Where are the dresses? And the sexy blouses?"

I pause for a second to ponder, tapping on my chin. "I don't think I've worn a dress since my senior prom."

Alex shakes her head. Obviously annoyed with me. "What did you wear the last time you went on a date?"

I walk to my closet and begin poking around. "Honestly, I

have no idea. It's been a while."

"Like, how long?"

"Three years?" I guess. "I'm not sure."

Alex's jaw drops. "Kristen. Are you kidding me?"

I shrug. "I've been busy."

"With what?"

"With work," I answer quickly. It's not a lie. I'm just not telling her which work keeps me so busy.

"Work doesn't keep you that busy," Alex rolls her eyes.

I cross my arms in front of my chest. "Are you here to help me pick out clothes or just to lecture me?"

"Both," Alex answers, pulling a black sweater and a pair of jeans from my closet. She holds them up to look over her choices. "This will work for now, since it's cold out. But you and I are going shopping before your next date."

I take the clothes from her and begin removing them from the hangers. "Let's see if I get through the first date before we get too worried about going on a shopping spree."

* * *

It's 7:00 on the dot when Dustin knocks at the front door. I close the book I'm reading and lift Jinx from my lap before making my way to the door. I'm so nervous I feel like I could throw up all over my porch, but I take a deep breath and open the door, trying my best to play it off.

"Hi," Dustin looks me up and down appreciatively. "You look beautiful."

I look down at myself, trying to remember what I'm even wearing. To me, I don't look any different than I do getting ready for work. But I smile and thank him anyway for the compliment.

"Hungry?" he asks. "I was thinking we would ride into Owen and get a steak, if that's okay with you."

"I would love that," I assure him, relieved to hear that we won't be staying in town where all of Fawn Creek can spy on us.

Baby steps.

With that, I grab my purse, tell the cats bye, and follow Dustin to his pickup that's parked in my driveway.

Dustin leads me around to the passenger side and opens my door, extending a hand to help me climb into the awaiting vehicle. I place my foot on the step beneath the door and climb in. If there is a graceful way to get into a truck this size, I haven't discovered it yet.

Dustin hops into his seat with ease, making me look like more of a fool for the way I struggled, but I'm sure he doesn't mean to.

Dustin's truck is newer and has grey leather seats. It's obviously a vehicle that was purchased within the last couple of years. Either Dustin has never actually driven this thing before, or he has spent an extreme amount of time recently detailing it. The carpet is clean, the interior is shiny as though it's been recently wiped down, and the cab smells like a mixture of worn leather and cedarwood.

This doesn't really align with how many times I've seen him in dirty work boots and jeans.

Apparently, he notices me inspecting the cleanliness of his truck. "I had it detailed today," he informs me. "I figured you didn't want to sit in my dust-covered truck."

I wave him off. "I would have survived. But it looks good. Smells great, too."

He smirks. "Thanks, glad you like it. It took me a few minutes to settle on which scent to use. Corbin bought me like fourteen air fresheners for Christmas. My stocking was overflowing with them. I have enough left to last for the next three years."

I let out a laugh. "Well, at least he got you something useful, I guess." I glance out the window as we leave Fawn Creek city limits.

It must be nice to have someone to exchange stockings with. Just another thing I've never realized I've been missing by being perpetually single. This realization hurts me more than I'm expecting.

I change the subject, hoping to soften the hurt. "Speaking of Corbin, he and I had a little bit of a chat today."

Dustin raises a brow. "I hope he wasn't rude to you."

I shake my head. "No, of course not. Corbin is always polite and respectful at school."

"Well, that's good to hear, because I don't always see that side of him." Dustin sighs. "I figure as long as he's respectful to his teachers, I can put up with the attitude he gives me."

I reach over and squeeze his hand. "Well, if it makes you feel better, they say that kids give their parents attitude like that because they know where their safe space is. He knows you're going to love him no matter what, so he's not afraid to push the limits a little."

Dustin lets out a groan. "That somehow makes me feel better and worse at the same time."

I let out a soft chuckle. "You're going to get through this. Teenagers are rough on their own, and Corbin has been through more than the average teen. But, he's a good kid, and he is going to be just fine."

"I hope so," Dustin responds, staring out over the steering

wheel.

The only sound in the truck is the radio softly playing an old country song from the 90s. I pause and listen for a second, trying to pinpoint the song as Dustin chimes in to sing along. "I know what love is, what's it to you?"

I smirk at the lyrics, how appropriate.

A year ago, I couldn't have even told you what I thought love was. Hell, maybe not even a month ago. Maybe I would have said it was something unreachable and unsustainable. Something that is meant for some, but not all.

And most certainly not meant for me.

But now? It's different.

Of course, I'm not saying I'm in love with Dustin.

Nor can I say I ever will be, but I can say that I can see a tiny light off in the distance that looks like it could be something.

"So, what did he say?" Dustin asks, interrupting my thoughts.

I blink slowly. "Who?"

"Corbin. You said you guys talked."

"Oh, right." I shake my head. "Nothing profound. He asked if we were going on a date tonight, and I told him yes. I asked if that's okay with him, and he said yes. I promised him that the two of us going on a date will not suddenly mean that I'm hanging around all the time, cramping your guys' style."

Dustin reaches over and gently pokes my arm. "What if I want you to cramp my style?"

I don't answer, but I feel my face grow warm as I blush. He smirks, seemingly satisfied by my response, but he doesn't say anything. Instead, he turns up the radio just a bit, and we fall into a comfortable rhythm singing along to an old country song.

It feels like we do this every weekend, and I have to admit, I hope this really is the beginning of something real. I could get used to this.

After a thirty-minute drive, we pull into the parking lot of Tumbleweeds, a local steakhouse. We order our steaks, salads, and baked potatoes, along with glasses of sweet tea. The minutes turn into an hour as the two of us sit and chat about every topic under the sun. I learn about his job, and share with him about what it's really like to spend all day surrounded by teenagers.

Spoiler alert, it's not as bad as one might imagine.

After dinner, we leave the restaurant and walk out to the dimly lit parking lot. As we step towards the truck, Dustin pauses with his hand on the handle of the passenger side door. Then, he extends his other arm, wrapping it around my waist. He pulls me towards him and then gently kisses me before he rests his forehead on mine.

"Thanks for coming out with me tonight," Dustin whispers.

"Thanks for inviting me," I reply.

"One of the best things I've ever done," he says.

And I have to admit that I think tonight is one of the best things I've ever done, too.

Chapter 14

It's nearly 10:00 as we are driving through the streets of Fawn Creek towards my house. Dustin's arm and mine are intertwined on the armrest between us, and our fingers are interlaced.

It's been this way since we hit the highway after dinner. The radio has played quietly, filling the cab with 90s country music, and we have just held on to one another's hands while singing along.

This hasn't felt like a first date. It's felt like we've been doing this for months.

There hasn't been awkwardness. He didn't hesitate to hold my hand. Maybe this is the difference between dating in my thirties and in my twenties. Or maybe this is just due to dating a man who seems to know what he wants.

Whatever it is, I like it.

Dustin pulls his truck into my driveway, and the gravel in the drive crunches beneath the weight of the tires. I turn to tell him goodnight, but instead he jumps out of the truck and makes his way around to the passenger side door. He opens the door and offers me a hand so that I can climb down.

My feet hit the gravel, and I pause, sucking in a deep breath. His chest is against mine, our fingers are intertwined, and our faces are inches apart.

I begin looking for the words, but before I can speak, Dustin leans down and slowly meets his lips with mine. His hand lets go of mine, and instead, he grabs my hips.

I move my hands as well, wrapping my arms around the back of his neck, and pulling him in closer to me.

He leans into me, and my back meets the bed of his truck, causing even less space between the two of us. When we come up for air, I lean my head back as his mouth moves to my neck. When his lips meet my neck, my skin is instantly covered in goosebumps.

This feeling is dangerous. And for once in my life, I enjoy walking on the edge of danger.

"Do you want to come in?" I ask. "Maybe have a glass of wine?"

Dustin laughs softly into my hair, but doesn't respond. Instead, he takes a step back and leans down to kiss me one more time, but this time more gently.

"So... is that a no?" I ask, trying to hide the disappointment in my voice.

Dustin wraps his arms around my waist and pulls me closer. "Kristen," he replies, almost with a growl. "I would love to come in. But not tonight. Not yet."

I frown, but try to keep it playful. "Tsk, tsk. After all that talk about showing me the difference between kissing and making out."

Dustin laughs. "And I will show you. But not on the first date. What kind of guy do you think I am?"

"Better than I gave you credit for," I answer with a smirk.

And for that, I have to admit I'm thankful.

Dustin grabs my hand and leads me towards the house. I

unlock the door and push it open, but then I turn back towards him, letting the screen door close behind me. Jinx runs to the door and stands on his back legs, placing his front paws on the glass while he looks up at me.

I look down at my cat and back up at Dustin. "Sorry, I didn't get permission to stay out this late," I laugh. "He's not used to me being gone when it's dark out."

Dustin steps forward, placing a finger under my chin and gently tilting my head back. "Man, that cat is about to hate me. Because I want to do this again. Over and over," he says, before meeting his lips to mine.

"Me, too," I answer just above a whisper as we pull apart.

"Good night, Kristen. I'll talk to you later."

"Good night."

I step into the house and close the door, but watch through the peephole as Dustin backs out of the drive and makes his way down the street.

After that date, and most importantly that kiss, I will, for sure, be up writing all night.

In record time, I shower, change into a lounge set, and make my way into my office.

While I sip a cup of chai tea, I read over the last scene I wrote. Suddenly, I wonder how I've ever written any love story, considering how long it's been since I've been kissed the way I was kissed tonight.

I clearly had no actual idea what I was writing about. Suddenly, all I want to do is tear back through my draft and fix it all. Darren is nothing compared to Dustin, and the way he kisses Katie is nothing compared to the way Dustin kissed me tonight.

Instead, I make a note on a post-it to go back later and add some layering to Darren during my first round of edits. I have a hard rule: I never go back to edit until I have a completed first draft.

I may be breaking a lot of rules when it comes to Dustin, but that will not be one of them.

My time will be better spent adding to the story of my two characters falling for each other now, while I feel myself falling as well.

Much like I've been doing lately, I stay up late writing, adding to my story. Two thousand words later, my story is getting closer to being done, and I am barely able to keep my eyes open any longer.

I finish off the scene I'm working on, where my characters have finally decided to give in and kiss for the first time— see, it's not exactly Dustin and my story? And then, I follow my nighttime ritual. I blow out the candle, herd the cats from the room, and lock the door behind me. I have the entire weekend ahead of me, and thanks to Dustin, I love the way this story is shaping up.

* * *

Saturday morning, I wake up just before nine. I make a cup of coffee, settle onto the sofa with Jinx, and spend some time scrolling on my phone.

For fun, I open TikTok and type in "Maisie Bloomfield." It's been a while since I searched for my alter ego, and I can't help but wonder what the world is saying about her now.

I would love to say that maybe the excitement over Maisie is dying down, but my orders and page reads are still steadily climbing.

The first video that pops up is of a woman with curly blonde hair and big blue eyes, clutching Maisie's newest book.

"Hey, guys. This is Lynn, and I'm the co-founder of Happily Ever After Book Fest. As you know, I host one of the biggest and best book-signing events here in Southern Florida every winter. I mean, really, name a better place to visit when the rest of the US is freezing to death, am I right?"

I shrug in response, as though she sees me, which is almost as weird as the fact that she pauses while she waits for a response.

"Anyway," she continues. "I'm coming to you guys today because I am in desperate need of help. Anyone who is anyone has heard the name Maisie Bloomfield, and if you haven't read her feel-good novels, what even are you doing?"

"Writing them," I mumble to the screen.

She continues. "I am coming to you guys to ask, no beg, for any possible lead to Maisie Bloomfield. I would love to have Maisie sign at my event, and my readers would, too. So, if you can bring me Maisie, not only will I pay for her transportation and hotel stay for the signing, but I will also pay for yours. How is that for a finder's fee?"

I let out a laugh, but then close out of the video and search for this book event. Honestly, I've never heard of it myself, but I've also never looked much into author events. And this event is huge.

According to the website, over 1,000 tickets were sold last year. I love books as much as the next girl, but I avoid concerts and theme parks, and crowded cities for a reason. And that reason is people.

However, I have to admit that the idea of dressing up as Maisie and meeting readers would be exciting. Maybe I would pick up a flowery pink dress. The kind that would make Alex's head explode.

Perhaps I'd take her shopping with me to pick it out.

Or even bring her along to the event as my assistant? Would Alex even be up to something like that? What would Alex say if I called her up and told her the truth?

I rarely take time off work or use my personal days during the school year. I probably could manage to do something like this. Just once.

I shake my head. This is crazy. If I come out as Maisie, then everyone will know what I've been hiding for all this time.

But, then again, part of me can't even remember why I've been hiding this for so long. Would it be so bad to let the world know who I am? Would it be so bad to own up to who I am and what I write?

I pause, spending several more seconds looking around at the website. At the bottom of the page is a link to an author application form. I could fill it out. I could take the time off work. The idea of going to Florida sounds amazing, but the event is three weeks away, and right now I need to focus on my actual travel plans. Next weekend I'll be in Manhattan with the scholar's bowl team.

This is not the time to complicate things, no matter how much I'd love to spend a weekend at the beach.

* * *

"Well, there she is, our savior," my father announces as I step into the diner on a late Sunday morning.

It's just after ten o'clock. Right now, the diner is quiet and nearly empty. That won't last for long, of course. Soon, the four churches in Fawn Creek will end their services for the day, and the restaurants in town will be flooded with families in search of lunch.

Fawn Creek only has a few places to eat: a Mexican restaurant, Pizza Hut, a drive-through burger place, and my parents' diner, Red Maple. No matter where you choose to eat in town on a Sunday after church, you are destined to find a long wait unless you are one of the first ones there.

For whatever reason, my parents only had one waitress scheduled for today, and she called in with a stomach bug. Luckily for my parents, I spent all day writing yesterday, and I could use the opportunity to catch my breath.

"Yeah, yeah," I reply to my father as I pause at an empty table and tie my tattered old apron around my waist.

I've had this apron since I was fifteen and legally allowed to start waiting tables. My mom had it embroidered with my name and gave it to me for my birthday that year.

Happy birthday. You may now officially clean up after people for the rest of your life.

Dad eyes my apron and scowls. "Kristen, when are you going to get rid of that ratty old apron? I told you, I have new ones in the office. Go grab one of those."

I pull the apron strings tight and stick out my bottom lip.

"No. This one has my name on it. It's special."

"I'm surprised it's still in one piece after fifteen years," my mom chimes in. "I have to replace mine at least once every two years, or my tips fall through the holes that form in the pockets."

I smirk. "Well, I'm not going to say I haven't repaired it a million times. When I was in high school, the Home EC teacher showed me how to fix it, so now I repair it every couple of years."

"You need to retire it," Dad chuckles.

"Well, I probably need to just hang it up for good, but where would you be without me?"

"Lost," mom answers.

I shake my head. "Well, you'd better come up with a backup plan for next weekend. I'll be out of town."

"Oh yeah, that school trip," Dad shakes his head as he takes a seat behind the cash register. "I still can't believe they talked you into that."

"That makes two of us," I confirm. "But, I have to admit I'm enjoying coaching the kids. They are a fun group."

Mom takes a seat in an empty booth, in front of a tub of silverware that needs to be rolled. I join her.

"Are you the only adult going?" she asks.

I shake my head, "No."

She raises a brow. "Are you going with another teacher?"

I focus my line of sight on the work at hand. "No, it's a parent that's coming. He will be in charge of staying with the boys, and I'll be with the girls."

"Oh, so a man is going?" She leans in as though she's ready for some juicy gossip. "Anyone I know?"

I pause for a second to take a deep breath. Here we go again with her digging into my dating life.

"Maybe Dustin Crenshaw, for example?" Mom asks with a slight smirk.

She already knows. Of course, she already knows. Word doesn't take long to get around Fawn Creek.

I let out a heavy sigh. "Perhaps."

Mom smiles triumphantly as she adds a roll of silverware to the pile in front of her. "How long have you two been seeing each other?"

"Not long," I wave her off. "I mean, we've only gone on one date. I don't know if you could even call that seeing each other?"

"Are you counting when you were sucking face in the high school parking lot as a date?" she asks, much too nonchalantly.

"Mother!" I gasp.

She shrugs. "I don't know why you're the shocked one. You did it, not me."

I feel my face grow warm, and I don't need to check my reflection in the napkin dispenser on the table to know that I'm blushing.

"We weren't sucking face."

My dad chimes in. "That's not what we heard."

I roll my eyes. "Well, you can't believe everything you hear."

Mom finishes her task and folds her hands in front of her. "Anyway. Whatever you want to call it doesn't matter. What matters is, are you happy?"

I pause, considering the question. "Yeah. I am."

"Then that's all that matters," she says, reaching across the table to squeeze my hand. "That's all I want for you. And for what it's worth, I like him. He's a nice guy. He comes in here a lot for lunch. He always tips well and is kind to the wait staff... and most importantly, he's patient. You deserve someone good, and I think you've found it."

I nod and look at the door, where a family of five dressed in their Sunday best is walking in. "I hope you're right, Mama."

"I always am."

Chapter 15

"Alright, is this everyone?" I ask as the kids gather in the parking lot in front of me. After a quick headcount, I determine we are missing one. "Where's Heather?"

Just as the words leave my mouth, Heather's voice calls out from behind me. I turn to find her running towards us from the school, dragging a giant suitcase along behind her. The bag has to be almost as tall as she is.

"Sorry, I was parked on the other side of the school," she explains. "The janitor let me in the back door so I wouldn't have to drag my bag all the way around the building."

Dustin picks up the suitcase by the handle and lets out a dramatic groan. "What the heck do you have packed in here? Bricks?"

Heather shrugs. "Just clothes, makeup, shoes.... a couple of books. Oh! And my weighted blanket."

I blink slowly. "You packed a weighted blanket?"

"I can't sleep without it," she answers defensively. "If it's too much, I can leave it in my car, but I seriously won't sleep, and then I won't be of any use to anyone at the competition."

Dustin and I exchange a look.

"It's fine," he assures me, as well as the rest of the gang. "I'll just have to do some rearranging in the back of the van.

You guys go ahead and get in so you can fight over your seating arrangements. I'll take care of this."

The kids follow his direction, walking around to the side of the van and climbing inside one by one.

I turn to Dustin with a frown. "I thought the van was going to be overkill, but I did not account for teenage girls and their overpacking skills. Now, I'm worried that there won't be enough room."

He shakes his head and chuckles as he works to pull the mountain of duffel bags from the back of the van and piles them at his feet.

"I can do this if you want me to," I offer. "I know you didn't volunteer to deal with lifting a bunch of heavy bags."

"Hey, I told you it's okay," he assures me. "I volunteered to come help you. That means, if something needs to be done, tell me, and I'll take care of it."

Dustin finishes restacking the bags and closes the back door of the van before turning to look at me. His eyes focus intently on mine. "I mean it. I know that you can handle everything on your own, but just because you can doesn't mean you have to."

I chew on my bottom lip for a beat and then nod in agreement. "Okay, but so that you know, I'm not great at asking for help. I've done things on my own for a long time, and I've made it work."

"I can tell," he shrugs. "Don't worry, I am going to do everything I can to change that."

"It's not going to be easy," I warn him. "In fact, this entire trip is probably going to be a lot to take in. You've got your work cut out for you."

Dustin steps towards me, lowering his voice. "The hardest thing about this trip is going to be going all weekend without kissing you. But, I promise to be on my best behavior."

His words cause those butterflies I've been feeling lately to flutter in my stomach once again.

"We will make up for it later," I respond.

"I'm going to hold you to that."

With that, I make my way around to the driver's seat of the van and climb inside. I glance in the rearview mirror to look at the kids, trying to assess whether or not they were watching Corbin's dad, and I flirt in the parking lot. Luckily for me, they all seem to be blissfully unaware, their faces buried in their phones.

Whew.

"Okay, you guys. We are ready to hit the road. This is your last chance to go to the bathroom for at least an hour and a half. Does anyone need to go?"

I watch as all the heads in the seats behind me shake no.

I look at Dustin teasingly. "What about you?"

He holds up both hands. "I'm good."

Satisfied with their answers, I nod. "Okay, if everyone is buckled, let's hit the road."

Within minutes, we are on the highway, headed away from Fawn Creek and towards the weekend that I have been anxiously awaiting for the past month.

I steal a glance at Dustin and then turn my focus back to the road, but it doesn't go unnoticed.

"Need something?" He asks, as though he is ready to spring into action.

I shake my head. "No. I couldn't help but notice that you are doing a great job getting settled into your role as passenger princess." I tease. "All I need from you is to be the DJ once 98.5 turns to static. Oh, and to warn me if I'm about to side swipe someone."

Dustin winces dramatically. "So, are you telling me that I signed up to meet my demise in a van full of teenagers, potentially?"

I shrug, looking out over the steering wheel. "I mean, would you really want to go out any other way? It'll probably be less painful than listening to all six kids watching TikTok at the same time." I glance in the rearview mirror towards the teens sitting behind me. "I know I put headphones on your packing lists. Use them or turn down your volume."

"We're making a TikTok," Heather explains. "It's going to be hilarious."

I shake my head. "Are you all making different TikToks at the same time or what? There are too many sounds in this van at one time, and it's too early in this trip to drive me insane."

Kaci jumps in, taking her team captain role very seriously. "Okay. She's right. Let's take turns. We can each film one at a time. Mine first, then Heather's, then Corbin, and then the boys in the back."

Corbin snorts. "I do not make TikToks. You guys go ahead and knock yourselves out. Just leave me out of it. "

"Corbin, please make them with us?" Kaci whines. "I promise I won't make you dance or anything stupid."

I watch in the rearview as Corbin stares at Kaci, considering her request. The tension in the van is already thick enough to cut with a knife.

"Come on, Corbin. We can't make videos without the whole team. It's just a little lip syncing." Heather chimes in.

Corbin rolls his eyes and lets out a dramatic sigh. "Fine."

The kids busy themselves with recording their videos, while I lean forward and turn up the radio to drown out their noise.

The station has already turned to static.

I turn to Dustin. "Alright, DJ. It's your time to shine."

"What would you like to listen to?" Dustin asks.

"Country is probably safest," I shrug. "Personally, I prefer to listen to divorced dad rock, but I don't know how many of these kids will tell on me for playing music with bad words."

Dustin raises a brow. "Divorced dad rock?"

I shrug. "Yeah, you know. Nickelback, Creed, Three Doors Down... All the good 2000s rock music."

Kaci, the ever-so-helpful one, chimes in again. "Oh, like the stuff on the oldies station?"

I grip the steering wheel and glare at her in the rearview mirror. "No. Girl, how old do you think I am?"

Kaci shrugs. "I don't know. Thirty-something? I know that my dad listens to Nickelback, and they play that a lot on the oldies station."

I take a deep breath and count to five, allowing myself to pause for a beat before saying something I regret. Then, I turn my attention back to Dustin. "Country is fine. 90s country is a great way to annoy the kids if you can find it."

Dustin chuckles as he flips through the stations. "Well, it just so happens that annoying kids is one of my favorite hobbies. Just ask Corbin." Dustin laughs.

He settles on a country station and turns to look at me as *Man, I Feel Like A Woman* by Shania Twain flows from the speakers. Then, he begins singing along, loudly and proudly.

Corbin is definitely going to kill him on this trip. But, at least it'll be entertaining in the meantime.

"Wow," I laugh. "You are an incredibly talented singer."

I steal a glance at Corbin in the rearview. He's wearing his headphones and looking down at his phone. If he heard his father singing, which I can't imagine even the best headphones would have drowned out that screeching, he's not letting it be known.

Dustin smirks in my direction. "Thanks. Maybe if this whole Blue Collar thing doesn't work out, I'll try to launch my music career."

I nod, looking out over the steering wheel. "I think that's a great idea, honestly. Everyone needs a fallback plan."

Dustin nods as he takes a drink from the energy drink he brought along for the ride. "So, what's your fallback plan?"

Crap. I should have known better than to say that.

I look out over the steering wheel and try to ignore the fact that my palms are currently sweating.

One by one, I wipe them on my jeans before returning my grip to the wheel.

"You okay?" Dustin asks, with a raised brow.

I nod. "Yeah, just got a little warm. Hot flash or something." I try to laugh it off.

He gives me an understanding nod before bringing the conversation back up. "So, what's your fallback plan then?"

I pause for a second and think of how I should answer. If the kids weren't in the van, I would probably tell him about Maisie.

I mean, we are dating, and it would honestly be nice to share this with someone.

Anyone.

But I can't tell him with a car full of kids.

Finally, I carefully respond. "I don't know. Maybe I would try writing one day."

He perks up just a bit in his seat. "Writing what?"

I shrug. "Books... novels."

Dustin grins. "Like, horror novels?"

I let out a large laugh. If only he knew. "Yeah, something like that."

Chapter 16

I put the van in park in the hotel parking lot, and turn and look at the van full of teens. Kaci has her nose buried in a book. Heather is passed out in what has to be the most uncomfortable sleeping position. Her head is all the way back, resting against the seat behind her.

Corbin is on the other side of Heather. He is intently focused on a Nintendo Switch that's in his hand and hasn't seemed to notice that we are parked. Nash is also sleeping, but he's curled up in the corner of the back row. Next to him, Jaxson is wearing his headphones and staring at his screen, while Dillon is also probably sleeping, but I can't tell because the hood of his sweatshirt is pulled over his eyes. He's leaning against the window next to him.

Well, at least I hope he's sleeping and not dead, or that's going to put a real damper on our weekend.

Even Dustin is passed out. I may have been just kidding about him being a passenger princess, but he ended up executing his job flawlessly.

Well, the princess part at least. No one in the van was alert while I was bobbing and weaving through traffic, which was probably just as well.

At least I didn't end up side-swiping anyone.

Not that I know of anyway.

"Up and at 'em!" I call out to the van full of inattentive passengers.

Without waiting for a response, I open my door and climb out of the van with a loud groan as I stretch my legs. Even though we stopped halfway here to use the restroom and stretch, my body aches from sitting on the worn van seat for all that time.

Maybe I'm getting too old for long trips in the van. Or maybe my pain is from the way I felt my body tense as I was walking dangerously close to letting Dustin in on my secret. I don't think I relaxed for a second until we got to our first gas station stop, and even after that, I was very careful not to say anything to give myself away.

This secret is killing me.

The longer I live with it on my own, the more I want to tell someone, but I'm also worried it might have gone too far. Maybe I waited too long.

Of course, I'll have to tell Dustin someday. I mean, we just started dating, so we are getting to know each other, but eventually the truth will have to come out. This isn't really the kind of thing I can take to my grave.

At the rate that Maisie's popularity is growing, I surely couldn't marry this guy and hide the fact that I'm bringing home six figures a month. He's never going to believe I'm doing that on a teacher's salary, no matter how good our test scores are.

I think the hardest part is the fact that this isn't some dark secret. It's not something that will make him want me any less. I don't write about gruesome murders or romance that's so dark it'll drive you straight to therapy. I write love stories.

Sweet love stories with happy endings and relatable characters. Sure, those around me have inspired some of my characters over the years, but never in a bad light. And if I needed a villain, which I have over the years, I've always made them from scratch.

I haven't hidden this from the world because I'm ashamed or afraid of what people would say. I hid it because I never assumed it would amount to anything.

Boy, was I wrong.

I open the door to the van, and a couple of the kids at least look in this direction this time. Slow progress is still progress, I guess.

Slowly, as though they are the ones that were fighting for their lives in traffic, the kids and Dustin climb out of the van in a chorus of moans and groans. Finally, we gather our luggage and make our way inside.

"I'm hungry," Nash whines as we step through the sliding glass doors.

'Me, too." Kaci chimes in. "What's for dinner?"

"I saw a Texas Roadhouse just over that way," Jaxson says, pointing towards the highway.

The kids respond with claps and cheers as Dustin and I exchange a glance.

I stop short of approaching the check-in desk and spin on my heel to address the kids. "Do y'all have Texas Roadhouse money? Because the school is covering lunch for tomorrow, but dinner is on you. And I don't need you spending everything you have on one meal."

The kids nod in unison.

I'm still not buying it.

"My mom sent me with $100 and a credit card," Kaci informs me. "Just in case."

The other kids start chiming in on how much money they have. I raise a hand. "Hey, you're going to get us mugged in the parking lot. If you guys have the money, I truly don't mind," I shrug. "I just don't want to be stuck doing dishes because someone couldn't pay for their steak."

I know it wouldn't come to that. I'd happily cover dinner for the kids. It's not like I didn't have a sudden windfall that I wasn't expecting. But being their teacher puts me in a tricky situation. If I pay for them for one meal, I'll be expected to pay for every meal for every school trip for the rest of my life.

I may not have kids of my own, but I'm smart enough to know that you'd better not do something once unless you plan to do it over and over.

I get us checked in, and we make our way up the third floor to our rooms.

"Okay, girls, we are in 325, and boys, you are in 327. Everyone has ten minutes to get settled, and then we will go eat."

I didn't realize how hungry I was until the kids started to talk about steak. Now I'm starving.

"Yes, ma'am," the kids reply in a chorus.

I swipe the key card to open the door and let the girls into the room, as Dustin does the same for the boys. I'm just about to follow Kaci and Heather into the room when I notice Dustin hanging back, with a slight smirk on his face.

"I'll be right there, girls. You two decide if you are sharing a bed or if one of you is sleeping on the couch." I tell them as I hold the door open. "I am too old to sleep on the couch. Unless you want to listen to me complain about it for the rest of the weekend, so one of the beds is mine."

"We will share!" the girls both respond at once.

Satisfied with their answer, I let the door close. Then, I turn to Dustin, finally taking a deep breath and relaxing for the first time since we left the school. "Hi," I say, just above a whisper.

"Hi," he replies, reaching out for my hand.

I pause, relaxing just a little. "Well, you survived the van ride. Now we have to make it through tomorrow."

Dustin grins, pulling me close to him. I'm expecting him to pull me in for a deep kiss, but I'm surprised when he hugs me. Just before he pulls away, he plants a gentle kiss on my forehead. "Has anyone ever told you what an amazing teacher you are? These kids love you, and you are so good at dealing with them."

"Thank you," I answer, looking at the door as if they can see me. "I love what I do. And I really like this group of kids. They make my job a lot easier than it could be."

Dustin smirks, "Well, if you ever decide to go for that fallback plan of writing scary books, I hope you don't quit teaching. You're really good at this, and Fawn Creek is really lucky to have you."

"I'll do the best I can to manage both," I promise him.

And for once, I don't feel like I'm lying or hiding anything.

* * *

"Oh my gosh," Kaci groans as she leans back with her hand on her stomach. "I'm never eating again. I am so full."

"Never, you say?" Heather smirks as she barely holds open the top of her brown leather purse to reveal something wrapped in several napkins. "So, I guess you won't want any of the rolls I'm taking back to the hotel for our midnight snack?"

"Heather," I hiss quietly. "Are you really committing Grand Larceny on a scholar's bowl trip? And what would your mom say about you filling your designer purse with bread?"

Heather's jaw drops as though the dinner roll police are questioning her. "I.. um.. well, they were just going to throw them away since they already brought them to the table. Plus, the bag is a knock-off."

I shrug and offer her a smirk as I toss a French fry into my mouth. "Did you at least get enough for all three of us?"

"Oh, absolutely," she answers, the color returning to her face when she realizes that she's not actually in trouble.

Jaxson chimes in. "Well, that's not fair. How are we supposed to take ours home?" He pauses for a second to consider the situation. "Hey, Ms. Calhoun, will you put our leftover rolls in your purse?"

I shake my head and clutch my purse to my chest as though to protect it. "No way, kid. I can not take the chance of being banned from Texas Roadhouse. Not after that one time at the Waffle House."

The table erupts into laughter as Dustin comes back to the table from the bathroom. "Oh gosh, what's so funny?" he asks. "Or do I even want to know?"

Heather waves him off. "Oh, we are just talking about that one time that Ms. Calhoun got a felony at the Waffle House. Nothing new."

Dustin turns to me with a raised brow. "Are they joking?"

I shrug, stirring the last bit of the ice in my glass with my straw. "Maybe, maybe not."

"What happens at the Waffle House, stays at the Waffle House," Nash chimes in.

Before I can assure Dustin that the kids are joking, our waitress stops by the table.

"Anyone need any drink refills or to-go boxes?" she offers.

"Yes, two boxes," I answer quickly. Anything to get the rolls and stolen linen napkins out of Heather's bag. "And just the checks, please. They are all separate."

The waitress and Dustin exchange a glance. "Oh," she says, sounding surprised. "The check has already been taken care of." She motions her head towards Dustin.

I turn to him and raise a brow. "Well, that was very nice of you. And completely unnecessary. When did you do that?"

Dustin shrugs. "I lied about going to the bathroom. And, it was no problem. Now everyone will have plenty of cash to make it through tomorrow."

These kids are never going to learn to budget on a trip if people like Dustin keep spoiling them, but I'm not going to call him out for it in front of the kids.

I turn to glance around the table. "What do you guys tell Corbin's dad?'

"Thank you!" the kids answer in a chorus.

"Man," Nash mumbles, "if I'd have known I wasn't going to have to pay for it, I would have gotten a bigger steak or a virgin daiquiri."

I turn to Nash, sending him my patented teacher death glare.

"Their margaritas are really good here, too." Kaci chimes in and then turns to look at me. "From what I've heard, anyway. You should have gotten one tonight, Ms. Calhoun."

I shake my head. "As much as you guys make me wish I could have a giant margarita, drinking on the job is frowned upon. So, I'll have to make a trip to get one on my own after we get back. Goodness knows I'll need one by then."

The waitress returns the boxes, and I hand one to Heather. "Here, unpack your purse carbs, and put them in here like a normal person."

Sheepishly, Heather takes the box and unpacks her bag.

While she does that, I pile my silverware and napkin on top of my plate. Then, I instruct the kids to do the same. Apparently, some waitress habits never die.

Just as I finish, my phone vibrates in my lap. It's a text from Dustin. I look up at him with a raised brow and then open the message, being sure to shield the screen to protect it from wandering eyes.

Dustin: When we get back to Fawn Creek, let's go out for a couple of those margaritas—just you and me.

I read the text and smirk, and look up at him. He wiggles his eyebrows at me while I try to ignore the fact that I'm blushing.

"Are we ready?" Heather asks, standing from the table as she slings her carb-free purse over her shoulder.

"Yeah, let's go back to the hotel and get some rest. We have a long day tomorrow." I say, standing from my seat.

The kids walk ahead of me, and I pause to hand the waitress an extra tip before joining them. She looks down at the two twenty-dollar bills and then back to me. "Thank you, but the man who paid the bill left me a great tip," she assures me.

"I'm sure he did, but I wait tables too, and I know what a pain it can be to wait on a bunch of teenagers, so I want to give you a little something extra. Have a good night."

Before the girl can push back any further, I rush towards the door, following the rest of the team towards the school van. It's going to be a long night, and not because I'll be hanging out with a couple of teenage girls. It has more to do with the handsome and very giving dad who will be on the other side of the wall.

Chapter 17

After getting back to the hotel, the girls and I take turns showering, and we get settled into our room for the night.

By ten, the two of them are sitting on one queen bed, scrolling through videos, while I sit on the other bed, scanning through the TV Guide for something to watch.

I didn't bring my laptop, since it's only a one-night stay. I knew I wouldn't be able to get any privacy to write anyway.

The last thing I need is to get caught in Maisie Mode by Heather and Kaci.

Instead, I dig into my teacher bag and pull out a stack of papers to grade, with the sounds of TikTok and The Office playing in the background.

I get about halfway through reading one essay when the sound of Heather's gasp causes me to drop my red pen and prepare to spring into action.

I'm not sure what I thought was going on. Maybe she sounded like she was choking on a leftover roll and falling off the bed, but the cause of her excitement is much worse.

"There's a witch hunt," Heather says, holding up her phone to show me the screen. "Over that Maisie Bloomfield lady. This book influencer from Texas is determined to find out who she is and why she is in hiding."

I swallow hard. "I don't understand this obsession over who she is."

Kaci shrugs. "Who doesn't love a good mystery?"

"And what if she doesn't want to be found? I mean, if she did, she probably would have come forward already." I argue. "Give the woman some peace."

The girls don't respond; they share a glance and return to their phones. I shake my head and get back to grading, just as a text comes through from Dustin.

Dustin: Hey, I didn't think about this, but Sunday is Valentine's Day. Do you want to go out that day? I mean, I do owe you a margarita.

I read over the message and can't help but notice the butterflies are back in my stomach again.

I can't remember the last time I had a date on Valentine's Day or even the prospect of one, which is honestly sad because, for as long as I can remember, Valentine's Day has been my favorite holiday.

I know it's considered a Hallmark holiday, and you should show the people you love that you love them every day. However, the idea of one day a year when it's normal to buy flowers, exchange cards, eat chocolate, and make time for the person you love has always been something I've loved.

Even if it's been years since I've actually experienced it myself.

Kristen: I would love that. Or, if you want, you can come over to my place. I've been told I make a mean margarita.

Dustin: Deal. I'll bring the tacos, and you supply the drinks?

His offer sends a buzz of excitement through my body.

Kristen: It's a date.

I close the message and lock my phone, tossing it down on the bed next to me.

Now, how the heck am I supposed to focus tomorrow? I'm supposed to be worried about leading the team to victory, but instead, I have a feeling that Valentine's Day with Dustin, alone in my house, will be on my mind instead.

* * *

Saturday morning, my alarm goes off at seven. I wake up fully expecting to have to drag the girls out of bed, but instead I find Heather and Kaci standing at the bathroom sink. The countertop is covered in a variety of makeup, in the form of tubes, bottles, and palettes, as well as a couple of hot tools.

I stand in the doorway to the bathroom and rub my eyes. "What time did you guys get up?"

"Six," they answer in unison.

"Why?"

Kaci shrugs. "We needed enough time to get ready. There might be cute boys there today."

I shake my head. "You know we're at a Scholar's Bowl tournament, right? I don't think the kind of boys you are looking for are going to be in attendance today."

Heather rolls her eyes. "Smart guys can be cute, too."

Kaci chimes in. "My mom told me if I'm going to date in college, I need to date a nerdy guy."

I wave the girls out of the bathroom. "Okay, good point. But the smart ones are probably not going to be worried about your makeup. Now can I pee?"

Within twenty minutes, the girls are done playing beauty salon, and their collection of gadgets and goop is packed securely into their makeup bags. With all of our gear in tow, we carry our bags downstairs for breakfast before heading out to the tournament.

Dustin and the boys are already sitting in the breakfast area, eating plates full of scrambled eggs and cinnamon rolls, when we enter.

I drop my bag near the wall and instruct the girls to do the same, before practically crawling to the coffee pot. Dustin joins me just as I'm beginning to fill my disposable cup.

"Morning. How'd you sleep?" he asks.

I let out a big yawn. "Pretty good to be honest. I'm glad to see the boys up and moving. I was worried that I'd have to come help you drag them out of bed."

He laughs. "I was, too. They were all up yapping until one this morning. I finally told them that if they talked again, I was getting them up at four to go to the gym."

I let out a soft chuckle and shake my head. "I think the best part of that is the fact that the girls were asleep by eleven. I would have expected them to be the ones up yapping all night. But, they were up at six doing their hair and makeup."

Dustin laughs as he turns to lean against the counter, sipping his coffee. "Hair and makeup for what? The tournament?"

"I said the same thing. Teenage girls make no sense." I shrug. "But, I guess no matter if we win or lose, their smokey eye is going to be on point."

Dustin deadpans. "I have no idea what that even means."

I gently pat his shoulder. "Thank your lucky stars, buddy."

* * *

After a short drive to the school for the tournament, I park, and our team piles out into the parking lot.

First, the girls climb out with purses slung over their shoulders, making sure not to flatten the curls they lost an hour of sleep to create. They look more like they are getting ready for a photo shoot than a scholar's bowl tournament.

Next, the boys climb out to join them. Corbin looks like he might throw up from nerves, Nash might not have combed his hair, Jaxson has syrup on his shirt, and Dillon quite possibly slept on the way here.

What a group.

Dustin joins me, carrying the box full of snack bags that Kaci's mom sent. The food has to weigh a ton, but the way he carries it is so effortless. I have to admit, seeing the flex of his bicep causes me to melt just a little in the school parking lot.

Dammit, focus, Kristen.

"Alright, everyone, hands in," Kaci says, motioning for the team to form a circle. "Prairie Dogs on three."

"One, two, three... Prairie Dogs!" the team yells out in a chorus as they break out of their huddle.

Dustin and I exchange a glance, and I shrug. "Dorks," I whisper.

"Big time," he agrees.

We step through the glass doors of the school building, and immediately the reality —and absurdity— of this entire event hits me. For as far as the eye can see, there are teams of high school scholars, ready to participate in their sport.

Looking back at my crew and our matching Prairie Dog shirts with our blue jeans, I almost feel underdressed.

What have I gotten myself into? I thought the matching shirts were a good idea, but some of these teams have matching jackets.

If I'm going to stick with coaching, which I can only assume I'll be stuck doing until the day I die, we may have to up the uniform next year.

But I can't focus on that right now. I have to get us registered and find out where we are supposed to go.

"Wait here," I tell Dustin and the kids, before stepping towards the registration table.

At the table sits a thin woman with curly blonde hair. She's wearing a bright blue shirt with the tournament logo across the front and a sticker that reads "Hello, I'm Charlene."

"Hi. Are you checking in?" Charlene asks, her tone as chipper as her appearance warned me it would be.

"Hi. Yes, Fawn Creek High School," I say.

I barely have the words out of my mouth before Charlene gets to work, rapidly flipping through the stapled stack of pages in front of her. "Fawn Creek... Fawn Creek..." she repeats to herself as she searches, as though trying to remember. "Ah, there you are!" She snatches up her pink highlighter and marks us off the list.

"Your home base is going to be located in room 305."

Before I can ask, she pulls a map from a nearby pile and marks the room on the paper with a large, overly exaggerated circle in hot pink highlighter.

"That'll be right here. You guys are set to complete at 9:30, so you hang out in there and practice until it's time. Just be sure to be in place outside the auditorium by 9:15. If you are late, you forfeit the round and will be disqualified."

I let her hand me the map, and I glance it over. "This is quite an event, I guess. I've never done one of these before."

Charlene blinks. "I've been the local volunteer coordinator for the last seventeen years. In fact, I was the youngest coordinator to join the organization. It was the year after I graduated from high school."

"Wow," I deadpan. "I had no idea I was speaking to such an influential leader. It was an honor, truly."

I turn on my heel just as the look of quiet confusion crosses Charlene's face. As I complete my turn, I find Dustin watching me. All I can do is mouth "wow," with wide eyes.

"That sounded intense," Dustin mutters as I approach him. He eyes Charlene over my shoulder.

"She is practically Scholar's Bowl royalty. Show some respect." I scold him, somehow keeping a straight face.

Dustin can't help but let out a deep laugh, causing the entire lobby to turn and look at us.

"Anyway," I say, trying to avoid looking back at Charlene. I can feel that she knows I'm making fun of her. "Can you help us locate our room? I guess we hang out in there and practice until our meet."

Dustin, who has placed the box of treats on the floor at his feet, takes the map and studies it. "Lucky for you, I was once a Boy Scout, so I've read a map or two."

"You should have told me that a long time ago." I scoff. "I wasted so much of my phone battery using GPS to get us here when I could have had you lead the way. And don't keep me started on the missed opportunity to have you tie a bunch of knots in a rope on our way here... Or to have you whittle me something with your pocket knife."

Dustin raises a brow. "I don't think Boy Scouts whittle things."

I shake my head. "Why else do they need pocket knives? Of course, they whittle things."

Dustin sighs and hands me back the map before picking up the box from the floor. "Let's go find this room. First hall on the left."

We step into room 305, which is the Geometry classroom, according to the engraved plate above the doorway.

I slide my tote bag onto a student desk and look around the space. It's a typical classroom with desks and chairs and a kitty-cat *Hang in There* poster on the wall.

I stand with my hands on my hips and address my team in my best stern teacher's voice. "Guys, I'm only going to say it once: don't mess with anything in this room. They know who is in here, and if I find out that one of you drew a dirty picture on the whiteboard or ate the teacher's M&M's, I'm never taking you on another trip again. Got it?"

"Got it," the kids reply in unison.

Dustin sets the box of snacks down on the desk next to me and groans. "Kaci, what did your mom pack? Bricks?"

Kaci shrugs, "Last I knew, she had a bottle of water, peanut butter packs, granola bars, fruit snacks, jerky, sour candy, an apple, and protein shakes."

My eyes widen. "She knows that lunch is catered, right? We didn't need that much."

"I know, I know..." she replies. "But you know my mom. Snacks are her love language, so she really likes to go totally overboard with this kind of thing."

Heather laughs. "Girl, you are going to get the best care packages when you go away to college."

"If she lets me go to college," Kaci adds. "Sometimes I wonder if she is going to pack up and follow me there."

"She loves you," I tell her. "Moms are just a lot sometimes. I wasn't sure my mom would let me go to college either, but as long as I called her every weekend, she learned to live with it."

"And then you came back," Heather reminds me.

I nod. "I did. And if I hadn't, you guys would be here with a way less cool teacher, so count your blessings. Now, get situated, and I'm going to break out the flash cards so we can practice before mopping the floor with these other teams."

Chapter 18

As we leave our classroom home base and make our way through the halls of the high school, the tension is high. The halls are filled with parents who appear to be more anxious than some of these kids.

I suppose it's quite an exciting moment to find out if you did indeed raise a scholar.

I stand against the wall in the hallway, getting a good look at our competition while we wait. The opposing team, the bulldogs, stands across the hall from us, wearing their bright orange school shirts, and they appear to be doing the same thing.

As Charlene promised, our tournament time slot starts at 9:30 on the dot. The door to the auditorium swings open, and a small woman wearing a black blazer and a matching pencil skirt steps into the hall. She has what has to be the straightest and shortest bob haircut I've ever seen. I wish it were appropriate to ask her if her stylist used a bowl to cut her hair, as they did back in the 90s.

She clutches her clipboard tightly and ushers us into the room.

When we get into the auditorium, six of our team members walk on stage —everyone but Corbin and Heather— and take their seats around a heavy metal buzzer. The other team from the hall takes their place at the opposing table.

Dustin, Corbin, Heather, and I take our seats in the stands.

A bald man in a light grey suit stands to greet the contestants. "Welcome, everyone, to the Kansas State Scholars' Bowl tournament. Before we get started, I have just a few housekeeping reminders." He pauses to look from the kids to the audience. "Parents and coaches. I know this is a very exciting time..."

"Thrilling," I whisper to Dustin under my breath.

Dustin smirks.

The man continues. "But, it is very important that you stay as quiet as possible during the match. You mustn't distract these young scholars from answering the questions at hand. If you are not able to remain quiet, you will be removed from the room, but this may also cause your team to forfeit."

Corbin turns in this seat and shoots a look at Dustin and me, as though to warn us. My jaw drops.

"He's going to be a great dad someday," I whisper to Dustin.

He lets out a heavy breath. "Hopefully not for a long, long time."

Heather turns around and also shoots us a look.

"Sorry," I mouth. This is going to be a lot harder than I anticipated.

I am way too immature for this.

The announcer takes a seat but then leans forward to speak into the microphone. "Okay, first category, Classic Literature."

I settle into my seat. My kids know literature like the back of their hand, especially the older ones, probably because I've been forcing them to drudge through it since Freshman year. They certainly can't say I've never done anything for them.

"For ten points. This American author wrote *The Scarlet*

Letter, a novel centered on Hester Prynne's punishment in Puritan New England. Name this writer."

The announcer can barely get the question out before both Kaci and the male captain of the opposing team launch themselves towards the buzzer.

"Fawn Creek, you were first," the announcer says.

"Nathaniel Hawthorne!" Kaci exclaims with too much excitement for before ten in the morning.

"Correct. Next question. For ten points. This British author wrote *Pride and Prejudice*, a novel following the Bennet sisters as they navigate love, class, and social expectations. Name this writer."

Again, both teams reach for the buzzer and hit both buttons simultaneously. My eyes jump to the announcer to see who was first.

"Independence, you were first."

"Jane Austen," a boy with large wire-rimmed glasses replies.

"Correct," the announcer says.

I can't help but gasp at the loss.

Okay, maybe this is a little more exciting than I was prepared for. It's going to be a very long day.

* * *

"Okay..." Dustin says, holding up my phone to take a photo of the kids with our first-place trophy. "Scoot in just a little closer."

Looking down to make sure I don't step on any balloons from the insanely overdone white, gold, and navy blue balloon arch behind us, I squeeze in next to Heather. "Better?"

"No," Charlene answers for him, stepping next to Dustin.

"You need to be in the photo, too."

Dustin pauses. "Oh, I'm just the chaperone."

"No," I correct him, "you are a part of this team. Get over here."

Charlene takes the phone from Dustin, and he joins the crowd, squeezing in next to Corbin on the opposite side from me.

"Okay, I'm going to take several, so you'll have plenty to choose from," Charlene calls out as she takes a series of photos at varying angles.

"There you go," she says, finally handing the phone back to me. "Congratulations again."

I thank her and slip my phone into my pocket. "Okay, team. Are we sure everyone has everything?"

"Yes," the kids answer in unison.

"Perfect. Let's hit up a fast food place, and then we'll hit the road. I'm ready to sleep in my own bed tonight."

"Me too." Dustin agrees. "After listening to these boys yap all night, I might sleep until noon tomorrow."

"Ha!" Dillon laughs, "we had to listen to you snore all night, so you weren't much better."

Dustin scoffs. "I do not snore."

"Oh, yes, you do," Corbin chimes in. "Sometimes I can hear you from my room."

"That's going to be rough for you, Ms. Calhoun. If you guys ever get married, I'll give you earplugs for a wedding gift." Heather informs me.

"Heather!" Kaci hisses. "Who says we're even going to be invited to the wedding?"

Heather frowns. "Well, I think we will be! I mean, we are her team after all."

Dillon chimes in, "Oh, you think they are going to need our mad buzzer skills to exchange their vows?"

We've reached the van at this point, and honestly, I've heard all I can take. Dustin and my relationship is way too new for anyone to be discussing our wedding. I exchange a look with Dustin, who is laughing at this whole conversation.

Thanks for the help, buddy.

"Um, we are not going to be discussing any of this. Ever again. Get in the van." I say, as I leave the kids and climb around to the driver's side door.

I need to get through the rest of this trip without these kids embarrassing me in front of Dustin, at least more than they already have.

* * *

I pull into the parking lot next to Fawn Creek High just after 11:00 pm, and turn to look at my van load of sleepy teens. "Okay, we made it. Get out so I can go home and go to bed."

"Sheesh, so nurturing," Nash mumbles under his breath, but with an ornery grin on his face.

"Oh, my bad. Let me try again." I say. clearing my throat. "Time to wake up, all of you little sweethearts. Hurry up and get out of the van and go home so I can be that much closer to teaching you on Monday. And don't forget your trash!"

Dillon laughs as he works to slide on his backpack. "Nope, go back to the normal way. That was terrifying, and I'm going to have nightmares tonight."

Dustin and I exchange a glance, and I shake my head. "Can you believe these kids? They don't think I'm nice."

"Oh, Ms. Calhoun, we know you are nice." Heather chimes

in as she climbs out of the van. "But you're not sickly-sweet nice. You're like... spicy nice."

"Spicy nice! Yes!" Kaci agrees with a tired laugh. "I have never heard a better description for a person." I walk around to the back of the van to help Dustin as he unloads duffel bags and Heather's sixty-pound suitcase. The kids walk around the back to join us.

I hand Kaci her bag, and the conversation continues. "I'm just trying to decide if being called spicy nice is actually a compliment."

"It's one of the highest compliments you could receive, Ms. C., and we wouldn't want you any other way," Kaci assures me.'

Even through my exhaustion, that comment is enough to earn a genuine smile from me. Teenagers really aren't all that bad.

Kaci turns to Heather. "Come on. I'll give you a ride to your car so you don't have to drag that 60-pound bag around the entire building."

"Oh gosh, thank you," Heather replies appreciatively. "See you guys Monday!"

"See you Monday!" I repeat, watching them make their way towards Kaci's car.

I place my own bag and the trophy in the backseat of my car, the entire time shaking my head at the absurdity of this entire situation.

I didn't even want to coach this team. I wouldn't have volunteered in a million years.

Now, I can't imagine *not* being their coach. In fact, dare I admit that I'm actually looking forward to next year?

Within five minutes, the van is unloaded, and all the kids

are gone. Well, except for Corbin, of course. He and his dad offered to wait with me until the last of the non-driving kids were picked up.

As Dillon and his mom drive away in her dark grey minivan, Corbin turns to Dustin. "Alright, Dad. Let's go home."

"I'll be right there," Dustin replies.

Corbin lets out a loud groan. "Okay, but please don't have a repeat of last time."

With that, Corbin spins on his heel and walks over to the truck to climb inside.

As he closes the door with a thud, Dustin turns to me with a *What the heck was that?* look.

I shrug in response. Who can ever really guess what's going through the head of a teenager?

Dustin removes his hat and puts it on backward, and then steps closer to me. This new look causes my pulse to quicken. How did a hat position make him even hotter?

"Teenagers, man." That's all I can say, as I try to play it cool.

Dustin leans down and kisses my lips gently, but with just enough hunger to keep me wanting more. "It was hard to go all day without doing that," he confesses, resting his forehead on mine.

"Agreed," I confess before pulling back and then changing my mind and kissing him once more.

Corbin, who is still in the truck, turns the hazard lights on and off.

"I think that's his equivalent of switching the porch light on and off," I say.

Dustin lets out a soft chuckle. "Yeah, I guess I'd better get going before I get in trouble. Wouldn't want to get grounded before our date tomorrow."

Oh right. Our date. I almost forgot.

"You'd better not. You still bringing the food, and I'm making the drinks?" I ask, mentally adding to my to-do list to run by the store tomorrow morning.

"Yes, ma'am. How's 6:30?"

"I'll be here," I nod. "Now you really better go before Corbin comes and drags you to the truck."

Dustin lets out a heavy sigh. "Alright, fine. I'll see you tomorrow night."

I climb into my car, and Dustin waits for me to reverse out of my spot before driving away.

The drive across Fawn Creek towards my house might be a short one; it's only a few minutes after all, but it's plenty of time for me to spiral absolutely.

A man is coming to my house tomorrow.

It's been years since I brought a man home.

And not only that, but *it's been years since I brought a man home*, if you know what I mean. I need to shave and exfoliate. I need to clip and paint my toenails.

I need a bra and a pair of underwear that don't look like I bought them in an eight-pack at Walmart.

In addition to all of this, my house needs to be cleaned, my laundry needs to be done, and I need to grocery shop... And don't even get me started on the fact that Maisie has been in the back of my mind for the last three hours, basically dictating my next chapter to me.

It's going to be a very long night.

Chapter 19

The screaming of my alarm clock comes much too early on Sunday morning. I had good intentions last night when I set the alarm for 8:00, but now I'm full of regret.

When I got home, I was buzzing with excitement and anxiety. Knowing there was no way I was going to be able to go to sleep, I decided I'd knock out a few things from my to-do list.

My intentions were clear: start the laundry, empty the litter boxes, and quickly pick up the house. Somehow that turned into washing two loads of laundry, wiping down the kitchen and bathroom, picking up the house, and placing a grocery delivery order for this morning.

Generally, I try to only shop at Fawn Creek Market. In fact, I make a real effort to shop local as often as possible. Partly because after working all day, I have no desire to get in the car and drive to a nearby town to shop for groceries. But also, being raised by my parents, who own a small business in our community, helped shape my outlook on how and where I spend my money.

To a consumer, it may feel like nothing to travel out of town, go out to dinner, and shop at a big-box store. But, to people like my parents, especially when they were raising my brother and me, it meant everything when people chose to eat at the diner instead. It meant my parents might be able to buy me new shoes when mine were worn out, or buy my brother new jeans when he kept wearing holes in the knees.

Money spent in your community stays in your community.

But, unfortunately, the grocery store doesn't offer a delivery service that I can use for coffee, creamer, margarita mix... plus a black lace bra and panty set.

Thank God, honestly. There is a freedom in not having to look someone in their eyes when they hand you a bag containing a scandalous black thong... or three... I couldn't decide, so I ordered them all.

Maybe if this works out, I'll have a use for them. Perhaps, I'll make it a game to rotate all three, like some weird secret underwear Bingo game.

I mean, I already have plenty of other secrets. What's one more?

* * *

"Okay, Jinx. I have no idea what I'm going to wear," I tell my cat as he sits on my bed, staring at me with his head cocked to the side.

I really am going to take Alex up on her offer to go shopping with me. She's right. I have no date clothes. Well, except for the lace bra and panties that were in a plastic bag on my porch a few hours ago, next to my coffee creamer and a can of lime juice. But, I feel like answering the door without something at least over them would send a very strong message that I'm not quite ready for.

When I carried everything into the house and began to take it out of the bags, I nearly died of embarrassment. I still can not believe I had a perfect stranger shop for lingerie for me, and then another stranger brought it to my porch. But, I guess a couple of strangers is still better than being dropped off by someone who knows me.

At least, I'm assuming they were strangers. I will not be checking my doorbell camera to see if the delivery person was someone I know. My luck, it'll be one of my students from a previous year who's trying to earn a little money on the side. Or worse, one of my seniors from this year. This is one of those times when I would rather not know who has been on my porch.

Tired of standing in my closet in my scandalous underwear — underwear that I'm not really even sure Dustin is going to see— I finally decide on something that makes me feel like me.

I slip on my favorite pair of jeans, a wide-leg pair I bought just a few months ago and have kept in constant rotation ever since.

I remember the first time I wore these pants, I was so nervous about what the kids might think. If you want an honest opinion about your wardrobe, and let's be real, even if you don't, you can always count on teenagers and toddlers to throw in their two cents. Much to my surprise, when I walked into school that day, I heard nothing but compliments from all the girls.

I liked them because they are comfy and they look good on me... and because they reminded me of the wide-leg jeans I used to wear in high school. But they've stayed in rotation because of the way the kids at school hyped me up. It's nice to feel like a cool teacher every once in a while. Even if I secretly am not cool at all.

I've decided to pair my jeans with a hunter green sweater. It's a little bit cropped and boxy, and it hangs off my shoulder just a little bit, so I can't wear it to school. I wouldn't really consider it date night sexy, but it's better than a lot of my options.

Once I'm dressed, I stand in front of the mirror and look over my appearance once more. My dark brown hair falls just past my shoulders; I think my hairstylist, Sierra, called it a long bob last time she cut it. I call it long enough to wear in a ponytail but short enough that I usually leave it down.

Satisfied with how I look, because let's be honest, it's probably the best it's going to get, I leave the bedroom, shutting off the light as I walk out. Jinx follows behind me.

Next, I pause at the door of my office to make sure it is locked. I jiggle the handle, and sure enough, it doesn't turn. The last thing I want to do tonight is let Dustin in on my secret.

I'll do it soon, but not yet.

It's 6:28 when I sit down on the sofa in the middle of my quiet, dimly lit living room, relaxing for the first time all day... well, for the first time all weekend, really.

I pause to take in the room's decor. I've lived in this house for five years now, and over the years, it just feels so.... mine. I still can't believe I bought it all by myself.

After college, with my degree in hand, I moved back home and right back into my old bedroom. It was rough. Actually, rough is an understatement.

Now, don't get me wrong. I love my mom and dad. They are amazing and have done so much for me, but living with them again after four years of freedom was hard.

Mom was always asking about my dating life and sticking her nose in my business. I knew she meant well, but what twenty-two-year-old wants to hear that? And Dad... he comes across as passive and calm and so friendly, but every guy I even tried to date got the third degree from him when they came to pick me up for dates.

If I was ever going to get out on my own, I was going to have to really work for it. So, I did.

While I did come home with a degree, that didn't help much. Finding an open position at a school like Fawn Creek can be rough. When a teacher gets a classroom at one of Fawn Creek's schools, they don't tend to leave until retirement.

So, I did the next best thing. I took a job as a substitute teacher to get my foot in the door. And it worked. I knew before the board did that the English Teacher, Mrs. Faulkenberry, would retire after thirty years of teaching.

The day she broke the news to Gerald, I was waiting in the wings, literally. I was sitting outside his office. When she walked out, I walked in and begged him for the job.

I had already become the sub they could always count on. I was the first to take a job if one popped up. I never called in sick, and I was never late. My hard work paid off. I was offered the job, and I started as a high school English Teacher the following fall.

Even still, getting the job was half the battle. I was still living with my parents.

Rentals are scarce in Fawn Creek. The apartments stay full, and the few rental houses in town seem to stay occupied by the same people for years and years.

I talked to a local Realtor at the time, voicing my frustration about the lack of options, and she convinced me to buy a place instead.

So, I put my nose to the grindstone and worked like there was no tomorrow for a full year. I taught during the day, and waited tables in the evenings and on weekends. I continued to live with my parents, and I saved every dime I had so I could get a good down payment.

Then, the summer after my second year of teaching, I found my house. It wasn't much to look at. The siding was old and worn, and half of the metal windows were missing their screens. The carpet was dingy, and the interior smelled like it belonged to someone who sat inside and smoked three packs a day, but it had potential. And the sellers were only asking thirty thousand dollars, so I made an offer.

The sellers were ecstatic to get rid of the place, and they accepted the offer within twenty-four hours. By the next month, I was signing the papers, and then my dad and brother helped me start on the renovations.

Six months later, after a lot of hard work, sweat, and more tears than I want to recall, the house was done, and I moved in.

When I painted my living room walls a dark hunter green, my dad rolled his eyes, but I still have no regrets over my decision. I love them, and that's all that matters.

In addition to the dark green walls, the sectional sofa is a leather brown, and the floors are a smoky laminate wood floor. My mom assured me that it would be too dark and I'd hate it. But, five years later, I love my dark little cozy house. I love coming home and switching on my lamps and cozying into my throw pillows to read a book or watch a movie.

And then, of course, there is my pink, girly office. Sometimes I can't help but feel as though the office reflects my inner self, and the rest of the house reflects my outward self. I guess it would make sense. I keep that room hidden from the world, just as much as I contain my inner, soft, hopeless romantic interior.

Maybe one day they can live in unison.

A light knock on the door brings me back to reality, and I glance at the clock. It's 6:30 on the dot.

I take one more cleansing breath and try to calm my nerves. Maybe I should have taken a shot of the tequila on my kitchen counter because suddenly I am freaking out.

I open the door, and there stands Dustin. He's wearing a maroon-and-black plaid pearl-snap button-down shirt and jeans. He's wearing boots, but instead of his usual dusty work boots, these are clean and nicer; perhaps these are the kind of boots that he only takes out when he dresses up. But what I notice more than the shirt and the boots is the vase of light pink peonies in his hand.

"Hi," he says, holding the flower arrangement out towards me. "I hope you like flowers. These made me think of you."

I let out a soft chuckle. He is more on the nose than he realizes.

"I love flowers, and these are beautiful." After taking the flowers from him, I pause to lower my nose and take in the smell. "I'm shocked you were able to find flowers on a Sunday. Thank you."

Dustin shrugs. "Same. But, since it's Valentine's Day, the flower shop was open for a few hours this morning. I'll be right back. Going to grab the tacos from my truck."

I place the vase in the center of the coffee table and hurry back to hold open the screen door for him. He has his hands full of what looks like a giant pizza box, with a plastic grocery bag balanced on top.

I take the bag from the top of the pile. "Here, let's take these to the kitchen."

Dustin slides the box on the counter and looks up at me. The subtitles must be clear on my expression because he chuckles.

"It's not pizza," he says, opening the top of the box as if to prove it.

I peer into the box. It is tacos, like he promised. Twelve street tacos in the shape of a heart, with piles of onion, cilantro, and lime wedges in the center. "That is amazing," I laugh. "No one has ever brought me a heart taco before."

Dustin reaches out and grabs my hand, pulling me close to his chest. He kisses me deeply, with his hand cradling the back of my head. "Sorry," he whispers. "I'm just so excited to find out that I'm your first."

I throw my head back and let out a loud, appreciative laugh. "You're ridiculous. But, I like it."

He smirks. "Well, don't worry. There is plenty more where that came from."

Chapter 20

"Alright, I hope you are ready to have the best margarita of your life," I say to Dustin as I stand at the kitchen island. My ingredients are spread out in front of me, along with two glasses and a container of margarita salt.

Dustin, who looks completely unconvinced, raises a brow. "I don't know. Sprite, frozen lime aid, orange juice, and tequila? This looks like a recipe you picked up in a dorm room."

I turn to get a plastic pitcher from the cabinet next to my sink. "Well, at least something I learned in college was useful. Because that math stuff definitely was not."

Dustin shakes his head as he watches me open the can of frozen lime aid and plop the contents into the pitcher. "You? Don't like math?' He asks. "That's actually really surprising to me. I mean, because you are awfully smart. I just assumed a first-place winning Scholar's Bowl Coach was good at everything."

I try to fight back the urge to blush and concentrate on filling the empty lime aid can with tequila. I dump the can into the pitcher. "Well, I'm smart about literature and grammar and other things involving words. But numbers?" I scrunch my nose. "Count me out on those. I swear, once numbers get involved, I lose every brain cell I have. It's embarrassing."

Dustin ignores my math confession and stares at the pitcher with wide eyes instead. "That was a lot of tequila," is all he has to say. "I might have to call Corbin to come pick me up tonight. Talk about embarrassing."

I shake my head. "As long as we don't drink the whole pitcher, I bet you'll be okay by bedtime."

Dustin laughs. "I'm just kidding. I only live a few blocks away and can walk if I need to."

I pour about a cup of orange juice into my margarita pitcher and then place the juice container on the counter. "I just assumed you live out in the country, with your dusty pickup and all."

Dustin shakes his head. "Nope, staying at my parents' house until I can find a place for myself and Corbin. I thought finding a rental would be easier, and there's not a lot on the market. But, I admit it's nice to have the help. I'm still getting used to being the only parent. My wife handled a lot, and I'm just getting used to picking up the slack."

Silently, I open the Sprite and add half of the two-liter to the pitcher. Then I pick up a wooden spoon and stir.

I lift my eyes to meet Dustin's, and as I expect, he has a solemn expression. I can't imagine the hurt he's lived with from losing his wife.

"Are you okay? We can talk about her if you need to."

Dustin shakes his head. "I'm okay. I mean, I'm sure I'll never be healed or over it. But I've put a lot of work into therapy. Corbin and I both have. I try to remember the good times as much as I can."

"That's probably the best thing you can do, for both of you."

He nods solemnly before turning his attention back to the moment at hand. "It was hard. But, I've done the work, and one thing I know for sure is that I don't want my sadness to ruin the chance to make new memories. Corbin and I both deserve that, and it's what she should have wanted."

While listening to him talk, I salt the rims of our glasses and fill them with ice before pouring each of us a glass.

Dustin takes a sip. "Okay, I have to admit, that's pretty good. A lot better than I expected."

"The only difference between now and how I used to make it in my dorm room is the fact that I don't have to buy the cheap tequila anymore. I can afford middle-class liquor instead."

"Fancy," Dustin laughs.

"Thanks. That means a lot to me, coming from someone who lives with his parents." I say with a smirk so he knows I'm teasing.

Dustin laughs out loud. "Wow, Calhoun. Tequila makes you feisty."

"I'm always feisty," I inform him. "I thought you knew."

Dustin places his drink on the counter and reaches over for me. He loops a finger in my belt hoop and pulls me closer. "There's a lot that I don't know about you yet. But, I'd really like to learn."

I smirk, "Well, maybe I'll let you."

Just as we melt into each other, as our lips meet, my stomach joins the conversation with what has to be the loudest growl I've ever heard.

He throws his head back into a laugh. "Was that your stomach?"

I nod. "Yeah, it's possible I forgot to eat lunch today."

I won't admit to him that I was so focused on picking the right underwear that I never considered eating as much as a sandwich.

He kisses me once more and then takes a step back. "Well, it sounds to me that we'd better get you fed. There's plenty of time for this afterward."

Reluctantly, I agree. "Okay, fine," I say, as I reach into a cabinet and pull out a couple of plates. I hand them to Dustin and then grab each of us a fork.

Once we make our plates, we each take a seat on the barstools at the kitchen island.

The taco heart is a mixture of steak and chicken, and we each start with one of each. The plastic bag I carried earlier contains chips and salsa, so I open the bag and the two individual salsa bowls, and place them in front of us.

"So, speaking of getting to know you better," Dustin says, thoughtfully, after swallowing the second bite of his taco. "Do you have any plans over Spring Break?"

I pause for a second to think about it. My only plan is to stay home and finish writing this book. I have a self-imposed deadline to have the first draft done by Spring Break, and the book ready to go live by summer vacation. But I can't tell him that. So, I shake my head. "Nope. No plans."

His face immediately brightens. "Good. What do you think about going away with me for a few days?"

I bite my lip. "Oh, maybe. Where to?"

He shrugs. "I was thinking we could go to Arkansas and rent a cabin outside of Hot Springs. Corbin is going to stay in our old town with some friends in Texas during break, and I figure this will be a great opportunity for the two of us to spend some time together."

I don't answer right away, so he continues. "We could go fishing and hike, if you're into that sort of thing. Or, we could hang out in the hot tub, or you can sit around and read. Or hell, you could bring your laptop, and you could write."

His suggestion catches me off guard. "Write? Why would I write?" I ask, with a noticeable edge in my tone.

He furrows his brow slightly, obviously confused by the horror in my tone. "Well, you did say that you'd like to write someday. I was thinking maybe with some downtime, you could work on starting that novel we talked about."

Oh right. I did say that, didn't I?

"Oh, maybe so." I nod. "A few days away would be nice."

He pulls his phone from his back pocket and taps around on the screen. "The cabin is really neat. It's a cozy place with a hot tub and a fire pit. We could even go into town one day, and try those magical hot springs baths I've heard so much about."

I lean in and look at the pictures of the cabin. I have to admit, it does look pretty cool, and the idea of a spa-like adventure is very tempting.

I turn to him, narrowing my eyes. "You're not planning to take me out there and murder me, are you?"

He shakes his head. "Hadn't planned on it, no."

I pick up my taco and give him an enthusiastic nod. "Well, okay. As long as you don't plan to murder me, I suppose I could tag along."

* * *

"Those were quite possibly the best tacos I've ever eaten," I tell Dustin as I rinse our plates and load them into the dishwasher.

Dustin refills our glasses and smirks. "That's because they were made with love."

I shake my head. 'How do you know? You said you picked them up at the Mexican place downtown, right?"

"Yeah."

"Well? Did the chef tell you they were made with love? Maybe they were made with hate? Or worse, they could have been made with no feelings at all. That could have been just a giant heart-shaped box of meh tacos. And you'd never know it."

Dustin lets out a deep laugh. "I have a feeling they were made with love, since it is Valentine's Day and all."

I take a sip from my glass and wave him off. "Alright, believe what you want, I guess."

"I will, thank you," Dustin says, taking a sip from his own glass and looking around the kitchen. "So, what's next? House tour?"

Shit. A house tour. I love a great opportunity to lie about my office and why the door is locked.

"I mean, it's a small house, so there isn't much to tour."

He shrugs. "Well, then it shouldn't take too long."

I nod, trying to calm my nerves. It's fine. I'll distract him. This isn't my first rodeo.

I wave my hands through the air. "This... is the kitchen."

"The stove kind of gave it away."

I let out a heavy sigh. "Man, you are smart. I bet you probably would never guess that this next room, where the dining room table is located, is called the dining room." I say, as I lead the way.

This room is rarely used, so there's just the table, my china cabinet that holds a few books and knick-knacks in the glass cabinet, and cat food in the bottom, and a cat tree that my cats never use. Above the table hangs the black pendant light that my dad taught me to install.

I rest my hand on the table. "And this is my dining table. I refinished it myself. I don't believe that anyone has ever sat here to eat a meal, but I have one because otherwise you would walk through and hit your head on the light."

Dustin looks up towards the light and nods in understanding. "I see. Where do you usually eat?"

"Well, I'm so glad you asked. Let me show you," I say, offering a fake chipper tone. We make our way into the living room, and I point to the brown leather sofa. "This is where I eat. If I'm feeling extra fancy, I sit on the floor and use the coffee table."

Dustin shakes his head. "Very modern of you."

"Thank you," I nod, leading him down the hall. I push open the door to my bedroom. The two sleeping cats on my bed don't so much as open an eye. "This is my bedroom, but my mom said boys aren't allowed in my room until I'm forty, so you can't go in there. I'm only thirty."

Dustin snorts a laugh. "Okay, but in ten years, I'm going to see what the big deal is."

"We will see about that," I tease, "and the bathroom is right behind you. That concludes our tour for today." I say, trying to distract him. "What's next? Want to watch a movie? Drink another margarita?"

Make out on the couch?

Anything to keep him from asking...

"What's in this room?" Dustin asks, resting his hand on the doorknob of my office. I know the room is locked; I checked it myself earlier, but seeing him try to turn the knob still makes my heart race.

"Storage," I blurt out.

Dustin frowns. "Storage? You keep your storage room locked?"

"Well," I stutter. "It's not mine."

Dustin cocks his head to the side, obviously confused. "Why do you have a room full of someone else's stuff in your house? In a locked room?"

"It's my friend, Alex's. She just moved in with her boyfriend, and it's still a new situation, so I let her rent out my spare room to store her stuff. I keep it locked so there's no question about things coming up missing."

Dustin does not appear to be buying it. I have to change the subject.

"Hey," I say, quickly, reaching out to grab his hand. Gently, I tug his arm, moving us towards the couch. "Weren't you going to teach me something? I think it was the difference between kissing and making out?"

A sly grin spreads across Dustin's face. "Oh yeah, I was supposed to show you that, wasn't I? Well, consider class officially in session."

Chapter 21

The screaming of my alarm clock on Monday morning comes way too early. I hit snooze and lay back down, throwing a pillow over my face for good measure.

Who in the hell thought it was a good idea to drink three margaritas on a school night?

I should have used a personal day today. The school wouldn't have blamed me after I took on the task of the Scholar's Bowl trip. But if I were going to do that, I should have scheduled a sub last week, or at the very latest, yesterday.

My only option is to drag myself out of bed and go to work even though my head is pounding and my throat is drier than the Sahara Desert.

I stumble out of bed, into the kitchen to start my coffee pot, and then to the bathroom. By the time I'm back in my room, ready to pick out my clothes, I've downed two glasses of water and two ibuprofen.

One of the best parts about having a set color palette of clothing is that on days when I feel like crap, for example, if I'm hungover, the decision process is basically a no-brainer. I pull a pair of wide-leg black slacks with an elastic waistband from my closet and slip them on. Then I grab one of my many olive-green shirts; this one is a T-shirt, but it's fitted and professional enough.

I open the top drawer of my dresser, looking for one of my comfy but boring bras, and immediately see the black lace one I had on last night.

I run my fingers over the lace, and instantly I'm taken back to the makeout lesson that Dustin so kindly gave me on my sofa. While I'm still the only one who saw my new bra and thong set, let's say it was a lesson that I won't soon forget.

And now, I have to try to put it out of my mind. Instead, I have to go to school and somehow focus on teaching kids who have no interest in grammar or literature. Lucky me.

As I park my car in the staff parking lot, I watch Alex and Noah walking down the sidewalk, hand in hand. Seeing my friend makes me remember the little white lie I told Dustin last night.

I don't know why I didn't just tell him about the office. I could have shown him. I didn't even have to give him all the information about what I do in there. But instead, I panicked and lied.

Thankfully, at least it's not like Alex and Dustin are friends, and he's not going to ask her to rent a room from me.

Right?

I step through the front door of the school and wave hello to the secretary, Sharon.

"Ms. Calhoun?" she calls out upon seeing me. "Do you have the keys to the van? Gerald needs it today."

The van! Of course. So much has happened in the last few days that I forgot I had the keys to a school vehicle in my bag. I place my bag on the counter and fish around inside, locating the keys.

I hand the keys to Sharon and force a smile; my head still

aches a bit, but the medicine took the edge off at least. "We won, by the way, first place. I'll bring the trophy in later today. It's in my car."

"Congratulations," Sharon says, but with a frown. "No offense, but you look like crap."

"Thank you, that's the nicest thing anyone has said to me all day," I say with a raised brow. "But, you are the first person I've spoken to."

Sharon is still frowning. "You're not sick, are you? Flu B is going around."

I put my hands on my hips. "Flu B is always going around. But, no, I just stayed up a little too late last night. I'm fine. Nothing a copious amount of caffeine can't fix." I wave her off. "And speaking of, I need to get to my room and get my coffee pot going before the kids start to show up. I'll see you later."

Without waiting for her response, I sling my bag back over my shoulder and step into the hallway. Alex and Noah, the lovebirds, are standing in the main hall. Carefully, I step towards them.

Alex greets me with a wide smile. "Hey! How was your trip? And your Valentine's Day date?" she adds, wiggling her eyebrows.

I had sent her a text yesterday during my internal panic to ask for advice.

She just told me to be myself. It's like she doesn't even know me. There's no way I was in that much of a hurry to scare this guy off.

Noah perks up. "With Dustin?"

I let out a heavy sigh. "Yes, with Dustin."

The mention of his name once again makes me panic about my white lie.

"Nice," Noah nods his head. "I'll have to give him crap tomorrow when he comes over for poker night."

"Poker night?" I ask, looking between Alex and Noah.

"Yeah," Alex answers. "Usually it's a guy's night, but Noah's friend Jon can't make it. He's a probation officer and said it has something to do with needing to travel out of town for court. So, Noah is going to teach me to play."

Perfect. Not only will Alex be talking to Dustin, but she will be hanging out with him tomorrow, and I'm sure I'll come up. And so will the storage room.

Now I get to cover up a lie with a lie. This is getting ridiculous.

"Hey, Alex. I have a favor to ask about that." I say, chewing on my bottom lip.

"Sure, anything," Alex assures me. And I believe her, she has only been in Fawn Creek for a semester, but she has quickly become my best friend. "What's up?"

I take a deep breath. "Last night, Dustin asked me about my guest room. I keep it locked up, and he was asking what was inside. So, I might have told him that you rent that room to keep your spare stuff in it."

Noah frowns. "What spare stuff? Alex moved to Fawn Creek in a Mini Cooper."

I nod. "That is correct, but Dustin doesn't know that."

Alex lowers her voice. "I don't understand. Why are we lying about what's in your guest room?"

I grimace. "You remember that episode of Friends? When Monica had the closet that was so full of stuff that when she opened it, it was like an avalanche?"

Alex raises a brow. "Yes, I remember that episode. But Kristen, I'm shocked to hear that about you. I've been to your house, and it's so clean and organized."

"Well, now you know why. All of my clutter is in that room." I admit with a sigh. "I plan to clean it up this summer and get rid of it all. I need time. Can you cover for me, please? It's so embarrassing."

Alex and Noah exchange another look. Noah shrugs. "What'll it hurt?"

Alex blinks slowly. "I'm a terrible liar. If he asks me point-blank, I might accidentally make this worse."

My poor friend, I can not believe I dragged her into this.

"I'm sorry, and I'll never ask you to cover for me again. I promise."

Alex nods. "Okay. Don't worry. I'll manage. It's just one poker night."

"It's just one poker night," I repeat. "I owe you one."

* * *

By the end of the day, my headache is gone, but the guilt of asking Alex to lie for me is eating me alive.

When I started writing as Maisie, this was all so easy. I didn't have anyone to hide it from. No one came to my house regularly or tried to get into my spare room. I wasn't dating anyone, and I didn't really have any friends. My brother and his family moved out of town, and they avoided coming over when they lived here because he is allegedly allergic to cats. My parents don't even come over that often, and when they do, they don't tend to poke around in my business.

But now, it's different. Now, I have people in my life, and it's getting harder to contain my secret.

Months ago, when Alex and Noah started dating, I thought I was going to have to panic empty and paint that room.

Alex was renting a room from Noah's aunt, and she freaked out and considered breaking up with him for no good reason, mind you.

Anyway, she asked if she could stay with me. I, of course, would have let her. As I said, she's my only friend. I would do anything for her.

Luckily, I talked her off the ledge before she could make a rash decision, and she never needed to move in. I should have known then I was playing with fire.

And now, there's Dustin. He's such a great guy that it physically hurts to lie to him the way that I have been.

I have to come clean. Sooner rather than later.

Maybe I'll finish this draft and show it to him. It would probably be nice for me to give him a heads-up that the male lead is modeled after him, and I can't do that while I'm in the drafting stage. My first drafts are always garbage, and they are for my eyes only.

I already had a goal to finish this draft before we go to the cabin. So, I will work harder than ever to meet my deadline.

That settles it.

I'll bring my laptop, and I'll show him. I'll tell him while we're there, and finally I can quit living with this stupid, stupid secret. This will be all over soon. All I have to do is wait for Spring Break.

* * *

Tuesday evening, after school, I follow my usual schedule. Come home. Feed the cats. Shower off the germs that I picked up at school and settle into my office for a writing session.

Lessons in Love is still coming along nicely. I'm still adding words to the story faster than I ever have, and I'm falling more and more in love with Katie and Darren every day.

I have to admit, I'm falling hard for Dustin, too. Maybe not love, of course, it's too new to call it that. But it's definitely something. Something I've never experienced before, and honestly, something I'm excited to see progress further.

It's just after 6:30 when I finish my writing sprint and leave my pink, girly writing cave to go to the kitchen and hunt for food. I settle on the last two remaining street tacos —you couldn't have paid me to eat them, or really anything other than bread last night for dinner — and I side-eye the pitcher containing the rest of the leftover margarita mix. I should dump it down the drain, but I hate the idea of wasting perfectly good tequila, even though I am nearly convinced that I'm never going to drink again.

I heat my tacos and walk to the living room, taking a seat on the couch. Picking up the remote, I turn on the TV in search of something mindless to watch, but before I can settle on anything or even take a bite of my taco, my phone starts to ring.

I let out a groan. Please don't let it be my parents needing someone to work tonight. I'm still trying to recover from my weekend trip with the Scholar's Bowl team and, of course, nursing my hangover all day yesterday.

Getting older sucks. I remember when I could go to the bar and then wake up to work the morning shift at the diner without batting an eye. Now, it takes me 72 hours to recover from drinking three margaritas.

I pick up my phone and look at the caller screen.

It's Alex.

Shit. Alex is at poker night with the guys. What if she let it slip that I lied to Dustin? What if she caved? She did say that she's a terrible liar.

Quickly, I swipe my finger across the answer button. "Hello?" I answer. My heart is pounding in my ears.

"Hey, you busy?" Alex asks.

"No, not really, what's up?"

"Hi, Kristen!" I hear a male voice call out to me.

"That was Noah," Alex laughs. "I have you on speaker, by the way."

"Hi, Noah," I call back. "What's up? I thought you guys were playing poker."

"That's why I'm calling," Alex answers. "We were wondering if you want to come over and join us. Another one of Noah's friends flaked out."

"He has the stomach bug," Noah corrects her. "And I don't want that."

"Me neither," Dustin agrees, calling out in the background.

The sound of Dustin's voice causes those familiar butterflies to return to my stomach. I knew he was going to be there, but I guess I didn't expect him to have arrived already.

"We don't even have to play poker," Alex says. "It's not like I know how to play, anyway."

"I'd probably have to be retaught, too," I admit with a laugh.

"We'll teach you," Dustin says. "I'm a great teacher, remember?"

I thank my lucky stars that Dustin can't see me blush through the phone. "Yeah, I remember. I'll be right there."

* * *

I lean forward across the table and pull the pile of chips towards me. "Thank you, boys. I'll be sure to spend this money on something real nice."

Dustin shakes his head. "Noah, did I mention how glad I am that we decided not to play with real money tonight?"

"Only a hundred times," Noah laughs. "Kristen, do you have something to share with the class?"

I pick up the glass beer bottle next to me and take a sip. "Nope. Dustin is obviously just a very good teacher."

Alex and I share a glance, and she smirks, giving me away.

Dustin jumps to his feet with a big grin on his face. "You dirty cheater."

I continue stacking my chips. "I don't know what you're talking about. You are just that good of a teacher." I shrug. "Have you ever thought about joining the local school district? We could use people like you."

Dustin lets out a heavy groan; he's not buying it.

I roll my eyes dramatically. "Okay, it is possible that I have played before once or twice."

"Once or twice?" Noah repeats.

"Or a couple of zillion," I shrug. "I spent a lot of late nights hanging out at the diner with my parents as a kid. My dad and his friends used to commandeer the back table of the diner on Wednesday nights, when business was the slowest. And they might have taught me a thing or two."

Alex shakes her head. "I can't believe your dad taught you to gamble when you were a little kid. And in the diner? That has to be illegal."

"It probably was. But, those were some of the best nights of my childhood." I admit with a shrug. "We didn't get out much. They struggled a lot financially when I was younger, and even if they had the cash to take us to the zoo or on vacations or whatever, they couldn't because they had no one to run the diner."

Alex reaches across the table and squeezes my hand. "I'm sorry, friend."

I shake my head. "No, don't be. Really. My parents did the best they could with the time they had. I liked growing up in the diner. Besides, thanks to my dad, I kicked a lot of spoiled rich boy butt in college playing poker. That's how I paid for a majority of my groceries."

Dustin takes a swig of his beer and leans back in his chair. "Kristen Calhoun, you really are full of surprises, aren't you?"

You have no idea.

Chapter 22

The rest of the week flies by quickly, and before I know it, it's Friday once again. And it's time for our last Scholar's Bowl "practice".

"Sweet, pizza," Dillon smirks as he walks into the room and takes a seat in the front row of desks.

Nash sits down next to him. "Are we actually practicing today?"

"No," I shake my head. "The trophy is in the case in the hallway, and we are officially done for the year. This is your end-of-the-season pizza party."

"Nice. What else are we going to do besides eat?" Nash asks.

I frown. "I have no other plans. Pizza, pop, and cookies were the entire plan."

Jaxson takes a seat. "We could practice one more time for old times' sake."

Kaci interjects. "It's not really old times' sake if we just did it last weekend."

I shake my head. "No practicing for fun, please. I beg you. I am scholared out. Until next year, at least."

Heather smirks. "So, does that mean you are going to be our coach next year, too?"

I roll my eyes in fake disgust. "Yes. I'm going to be your

Scholars' Bowl coach for as long as the school will have me. I guess."

"Yay!" Heather cheers with a little too much enthusiasm.

The entire team turns to look at her.

"Sorry," she says sheepishly. "I get a little carried away sometimes."

I chuckle. "It's okay. I'm glad you're happy."

"I'm thrilled. Truly. This team has been my favorite thing throughout high school. I'd probably be doing online school next year if we weren't going to have a team. It wouldn't be worth coming in for, otherwise," she confesses.

I frown. "I hate that you feel that way. Heather, you're a smart girl, and as the only returning senior next year, I guess that would make you the new team captain."

This time, Kaci jumps out of her chair. "Let's have a ceremony. The passing of the buzzer. We can swear her in and everything."

Jaxson snarls. "That's not a real thing... is it?"

I shrug. "It's a real thing if we make it a real thing. I don't see the scholar's bowl police coming in here to stop us."

With that, after a brief huddle, the kids spring into action.

Kaci, being the leader she is, gives everyone a job.

Dillon- Lights
Nash- Music
Corbin - Media
Jaxson- Witness
Me-Official speaker
Heather- New captain
Kaci- Old captain

When Kaci says it's time, the kids spring into action as though they've been practicing this for weeks.

I'm a mixture of astonished, proud, and wondering if I'm being punked.

"Okay, Dillon, lights please," Kaci says.

Dillon shuts off one set of the classroom lights on command.

As soon as the lights are off, Nash presses play on the music. It's *Pomp & Circumstance*; a bit of a cheesy choice, but at least it's school-appropriate.

I look over and see that Corbin is actively recording.

I stand in front of my desk and wait as Kaci walks down the aisle of desks towards me. I nod and shake her hand. She stands to my right.

Next, Heather follows suit, walking down the aisle in Kaci's path. She pauses and shakes my hand as well, and then moves to my left. I begin the ceremony.

"Thank you, everyone, for joining us today for this joyful celebration. We have gathered you here to witness the ceremonial passing of the buzzer from one team captain to the next." I turn to Kaci.

"Kaci, I would first like to say that out of all the Scholars' Bowl teams that I have coached and led to victory, you have been one of the most influential scholars I have had the pleasure of working with. Your leadership skills will take you far, and your love of trivial knowledge will surely serve you well into your adult life."

Kaci nods, solemnly. "Thank you, Ms. Calhoun. It has been an honor and a privilege to not only serve this team but also lead us to victory at the state tournament. The friendships I have gained through this extracurricular activity will forever remain in my heart. But today is not about me." She picks up the buzzer from the desk and turns to face Heather.

"Today, I am passing the buzzer to a new team captain. A leader that I know will take our team just as far next year and add yet another trophy to the main hall, finally allowing us to show the athletic department that we are just as important as they are."

Kaci pauses for a second and then extends her hands and the buzzer towards Heather. "Heather Newbury. Do you promise to do everything in your power to support and encourage the Fawn Creek Prairie Dog Scholars' Bowl team? To cheer for them, whether the team wins or loses, and to uphold the reputation of our school?"

Heather nods and receives the buzzer. "I do."

Kaci turns to me and nods. "I now pronounce you, Scholar's Bowl team captain. You may now buzz the buzzer."

Heather's face lights up, and she looks my way for a nod of approval.

I never let them touch the buzzer outside of official Scholar's Bowl duty. It's loud, and with four high school boys in the room, we don't need any more noise than we already create. But it's a special occasion, so I nod, telling her it's okay.

She mashes her hand on the buzzer, and in the quiet of the room, it seems even louder than usual. I'm sure they can even hear it down in the office, but I don't care.

We survived our first season, and that's worth celebrating.

* * *

"Have a good weekend," I call out with a wave as the kids file out my classroom door at the end of our final practice. "Don't be dumb."

"We never are," Heather assures me with a smirk that makes me wonder the validity of her claim.

"What about me?" I look up at the source of the voice to find Dustin leaning in my doorway.

I grin. "Well, you're an adult, so I guess if you are going to be dumb, at least be good at it."

"Solid advice," he chuckles. "Dinner tonight?"

I steal a glance at the boxes of pizza lining the back wall of my classroom. "Well, I would say yes, but I may not ever need to eat again. I think I killed almost an entire medium pizza during practice."

"That means Corbin is probably not hungry either," he says thoughtfully. "I was thinking maybe the three of us could go out to eat tonight."

Corbin appears in the doorway, backpack slung over his shoulder. "I ate an entire pepperoni pizza by myself," he reports proudly. "Dillon said I couldn't do it, but I proved him wrong."

Dustin shakes his head. "I'm very proud, son."

"You should be," I chime in. "They were very dedicated. I told them that I didn't care how much they ate as long as they didn't throw up on the carpet. There's a lot I can deal with when it comes to teenagers, but bodily fluids are not one of those things."

"That makes two of us," Dustin laughs. "Okay, rain check on dinner then. Tomorrow?"

I wince as I move across the room to stack the empty pizza boxes so that I can throw them away in the dumpster. "I'm working at the diner all weekend."

And I really need to spend the time I'm not working on my writing. But, again, I won't be telling him that tidbit.

"Maybe one day next week we can grab dinner?" I suggest testing the idea, glancing to see Corbin's reaction. He immediately perks up.

"Can we go out for sushi?" Corbin asks.

I raise a brow. "Sushi? I never would have pictured you to be a sushi kid."

Corbin's face softens. "My mom used to take me all the time. And I haven't been since..."

The room falls silent. There's no reason for him to continue his sentence. We all know what he was going to say.

"I love sushi," I chime in. "I've been craving it lately, too."

Dustin sends me a thankful smile. "Okay, sounds like it's a date then."

"It's a date," I repeat, sliding my teacher bag over my shoulder. I move to pick up the stack of boxes, but in usual Dustin fashion, he beats me to it.

"Thanks," I say quietly.

"No, thank you. Truly," he whispers in return.

Corbin groans from the doorway. "Are you guys going to kiss?"

Dustin and I turn towards Corbin. I can't help but laugh out loud. "Not until we get out of the building."

Corbin sighs. "Well, let's get out of here so you two can get it over with, then. I've already been told I'm not allowed to puke on the carpet, so I guess the parking lot will be fine." He smirks as he finishes his little rant to show us that he's joking.

I shake my head and lead the two of them out of the classroom, locking the door behind us. We toss the boxes into the dumpster and make our way to our vehicles.

Corbin holds out his hand to Dustin, "Here, give me the keys and I'll start the truck, so I don't have to watch you play kissy face with my teacher."

Dustin lets out a groan, but pulls the keys from his pocket and places them in Corbin's waiting hand. As his son walks away, Dustin turns to me, lowering his voice.

"Sorry about him."

I wave him off. "He's fine. I deal with teenagers every day, and honestly, the teasing doesn't bother me at all. At least he's not being mean about it."

He looks over at Corbin, who is climbing into the driver's seat of his truck. "And thanks for agreeing to go get sushi."

I shrug. "I really do like sushi."

Dustin lowers his voice even more. "I don't. That was his and his mom's thing. I'm a steak and burger kind of guy."

I smile softly, "Maybe you haven't tried the right kind, yet."

"That's what Karina used to say, too," he replies. "I didn't believe her."

"She was right," I assure him. "We will find you something, I promise."

Dustin wraps his arms around my waist, pulling me in close to kiss the top of my forehead. "This parenting stuff is hard. I need every chance I can get to connect with that kid. I only have a few more years until he's all grown up."

"You're doing a great job," I assure him. "Karina would be proud. And I'm proud of you, too."

* * *

"Hey, don't forget, I'm not going to be available next week because I'll be out of town." I'm standing at the counter in the diner while Mom sits on a stool, working on next week's

190

schedule.

"Oh yeah... you're going on a little lovers getaway with Dustin, aren't you?" she asks, bouncing her eyebrows up and down.

I roll my eyes. "Yep. We are going to do nothing but be naked in the woods for four days."

Mom smacks my arm. "Kristen Marie Calhoun. Do not talk like that. We have customers in the building."

I dramatically rub my arm where she smacked me. "You started it."

Mom lets out a loud sigh and turns her attention back to her paper. "Take plenty of protection. Or don't. I'm ready for some more grandkids."

"You already have plenty of grandkids. Between Greg's three and my three cats, I would assume that Christmas is already expensive enough for you."

"I don't buy your cats Christmas presents."

I shrug. "Exactly. And don't think they haven't noticed. I've heard them talking about how Greg's kids are your favorites."

Mom lets out a groan. "So, are you saying you aren't going to give me any grandbabies?"

I shake my head. "Not if I can help it."

This causes her to put down her pen and give me her full attention. "And why not?"

I look across the restaurant and then back to her. "Mom, you do know that those cute babies grow up to become, don't you? They become teenagers. Sarcastic, smelly, messy teenagers. I work with enough of them every day to know that I don't want any of those running around. Especially if they turn out to be anything like I was as a teenager."

Mom frowns. "You weren't that bad."

I scoff. "I was pretty bad. You didn't know about most of it."

She holds up a hand to stop the conversation, "And I don't need to. Please, let me remain blissfully unaware."

"You got it."

Just then, a man and woman appear on the sidewalk outside. I turn to move in their direction to greet them, but Mom stops me. "Do you really not want kids of your own one day?"

I shake my head. "No."

"What about Dustin?"

I shrug. "He has a teenage boy. He probably doesn't want to start over again."

Mom smiles. "So, maybe I'll get a new grandkid after all. Just one that's mostly grown."

"Maybe so, Mom."

* * *

"Thanks for ordering me a drink," Dustin smiles as he slides into the booth to sit next to me after his trip to the bathroom. "Any idea what you're ordering?"

Corbin and I exchange a smirk, and Dustin catches us. "Oh gosh, what are you up to now?"

I shrug. "I went ahead and ordered your food, too."

Dustin blinks slowly. "I didn't tell you what I wanted."

I shrug and take a sip of my water. "I know."

"But..." Dustin starts to say, but Corbin interrupts him.

"Dad, you only ever get a California roll and then wonder why you don't like it. So, we are going to broaden your horizons a bit."

"We got a party tray," I tell him. "That'll make it easier for you to try a few things. And whatever we don't eat, Corbin can take home and finish off."

Dustin shifts uncomfortably in his seat. "Okay. I guess I can always hit up a drive-through on the way home if I need to."

I roll my eyes. "It'll be fine. I ordered some noodles and some cream cheese wontons, too. I promise, I won't let you starve. Just trust me."

As if on cue, the waitress comes in with our appetizers and slides them onto the table.

I pick up a wonton. "I could eat these as a meal on their own," I confess. "Actually, I do it quite often. Girl dinner."

Dustin shakes his head, picking up the wonton. He tears off the corner and settles into the seat a bit.

"So," I chime in, trying to ease the uncomfortable silence. "Corbin, your dad says you're going to Texas over Spring Break. Are you doing anything fun?"

Corbin perks up immediately. "Yes. I'm going to stay with my best friend, Garrett. I haven't seen him since we moved here. We are going to the pool and Six Flags. Otherwise, we are just going to hang out and play video games."

I can't help but smile as Corbin speaks, carrying on about Roblox and how excited he is to see his friend and the ultimate nachos that Garrett's mom makes.

When I first met him over Christmas break, he was a different kid than he is now. Back then, he was angry and displaced. He was mad at his dad for moving him here, and honestly, mad at the world because his mom was gone.

And I didn't blame him.

He didn't ask to leave his friends and the life he knew behind him.

He didn't ask to move to Fawn Creek, where the only people he knew were his grandparents.

And he really didn't ask for his mom to die.

It's been a hard year for him. But it's getting better. And so is he.

I think Scholar's Bowl has helped. Thanks to the team, he has friends at school.

All you really need in life is one good friend.

Sure, it's great to have a friend group or a handful of people you turn to, but you need at least one friendly face that you can spot across a crowded room. One person who's glad you exist makes all the difference, especially in high school.

The waitress returns and slides a colorful platter of sushi onto the table in front of us. "Enjoy," she says with a smile.

"We will," I assure her, as I look up at Dustin with a grin. "All of us will."

Over the next half an hour, the three of us enjoy our sushi feast.

Corbin dives right into the platter, not knowing or really even caring which roll is which, but the teacher in me knows that I have to treat this as a learning opportunity for Dustin.

With each new roll, I tell him the name, but I don't tell him what the rolls are made of. I asked him on the way here if he had any allergies, and he doesn't. So, that allowed me to order whatever I wanted.

But I also knew I couldn't do anything extreme. The reason for this date is to try to find him something he will enjoy eating, and hopefully that will open the door for the two of them to come on sushi dates together, just like Corbin did with his mom.

This is something Corbin needs in his life, and I'm going to make it possible for him.

By the end of the meal, it's clear that I succeeded in my

mission.

Our platter consisted of four different rolls, pre-determined by the restaurant. Out of the four types, Dustin found a new favorite: the Ninja roll, which consists of crab cakes, fresh salmon, cucumber, cream cheese, and salmon. And he's leaving with a plan to try a fried roll on his next visit.

"Okay," Dustin says, leading us towards his truck in the parking lot as he rubs his stomach. "You were right. That was good. I will definitely be back."

"See what happens when you broaden your horizons?" I smirk, elbowing him lightly.

Dustin grins and wraps an arm around my waist, pulling me in close. "I do. And I have to admit, I love all the things you're introducing me to. You're a pretty good teacher."

"You're not such a bad student, either."

Chapter 23

"Okay, I think that is it," I say, turning to Alex with my hands on my hips. Jinx is nestled in my arms, while he rubs his head against my chin. He knows I'm leaving, and he is not impressed. I lean my face down towards him, as if to hug him back. "You're going to be okay," I assure the feline.

Alex is at my house visiting with the cats. She will be taking care of them while I'm with Dustin at the cabin this week, and I want to make sure they know who she is.

Alex reaches out her hands to Jinx, who comes to her with no hesitation. "He's going to be fine, but are you?"

I swallow the lump building in my throat and give Alex an unconvincing nod. "I'll be fine."

Alex smirks. "You're nervous. That's cute."

This causes me to roll my eyes. "Okay, yes. I'm a little nervous, but can you blame me? I haven't had a boyfriend in a long time. And I haven't shared a bed with a man in even longer."

She gasps. "So, you guys haven't done it yet?"

"No, we sure haven't. We've gone on dates, and he's come over here. We have had many makeout sessions, but we haven't gone any further yet. We're trying not to rush things."

"He wants it to be special," Alex swoons. "That's sweet."

"I want it to be special, too," I admit. "This isn't like the last couple of relationships I've had. He's a good guy, and I really want this to work out. Besides, this is different from what I'm used to. I've never dated a parent of a student before."

Alex nods, holding Jinx closer as he melts into her.

That traitor, I thought he was obsessed with me, but it seems as though he will hang out with anyone willing to hold him. At least I know he won't suffer too much without me.

"Well, it probably does feel weird to date a man with a high school kid," Alex shrugs. "You aren't really old enough to have kids that age."

"Well, he is a little older than I am. He's thirty-seven, and I'm thirty, so it's not that bad. But, yeah, I am not old enough to have a teenager for sure."

Alex's eyes widen. "Do you think he wants more kids?"

Oy, with the kids' discussion again.

I shake my head. "I don't know. I hope not. I certainly don't want any."

Alex looks as disappointed as my mother did. "Really?"

"Really. I know it's expected for me to be all maternal and shit, but I'm not."

Alex laughs. "I can tell."

I frown. "How?"

"Well, for starters, you just said 'maternal and shit'." She teases. "So, does he know this?"

"I mean, I haven't even seen the man without pants on, so no, we haven't discussed this. One step at a time."

"Maybe that's a discussion to have on your way to Arkansas. Lay all your cards on the table before the trip actually begins, and then you can enjoy your vacation."

"Lay all my cards on the table," I repeat with a nod. "That's a good idea."

"I know. I'm pretty smart." Alex flips her hair over her shoulder dramatically. "So, what are you guys going to do while you're there? I mean, except for the part where you'll be naked. I don't want to hear about that."

I groan at Alex's joke. "Mostly, I think we are planning just to hang out. Dustin told me to be prepared to do some hiking. He's planning to fish, and I think I will try to get some reading done. And we're going to go into Hot Springs one day to try out a thermal bath."

Alex shakes her head. "I told you I don't want to hear about the naked part."

"I will be wearing a swimsuit, thank you very much," I say, rolling my eyes. "Apparently, the water that comes from the springs that feed the town is supposed to have healing properties. For years and years, people have been going there to do these thermal baths, so we figure we will try it out, too."

"Well, that sounds fun and very relaxing. You could use a little spa day."

"Agreed. Anyway, thank you for coming and taking care of my cats while I'm gone. It helps a lot to know they'll be in good hands while I'm on my trip. Maybe that will allow me actually to relax for once."

"I'm happy to help. By the way, speaking of help," Alex says, eyeing the closed door to my office. "Do you want me to help work on your hoarder room while you're gone? I love organizing."

"No!" I answer, probably a bit too loudly and too defensively. "I'll take care of it. Soon."

Alex frowns, obviously surprised by my response. "Okay, well, the offer stands. I'm happy to help you when you are ready to work on it. Sometimes having some help makes it go faster."

I nod. "I'll let you know."

I have got to come clean with this girl about my office. As soon as I get back from telling Dustin, I'll tell her too. And at least my closest friends will know my secret, and I can stop all this lying.

* * *

I stick my overnight bag in the backseat of Dustin's extended cab pickup and then climb into the passenger seat.

"Ready? Got everything?"

I look at my bag, then back at him. "I think so. If not, I'll manage."

Satisfied with my answer, Dustin nods and reverses out of the drive. "If nothing else, we won't be too far from civilization."

I shrug. "I've got my phone charger and my toothbrush, I can't imagine I'll need much more than that."

Dustin laughs and reaches for my hand, interlacing her fingers in mine. "I'm so glad we're doing this. I've been looking forward to it all week." He lifts my hand to his mouth and gently kisses it.

The way he touches me makes me want to melt into a pile in the seat of his truck.

"Same," I admit. "This will be a good chance to really get to know each other."

Saying that reminds me of the whole baby discussion that I had with both Alex and my mom. I grimace at the thought of having to have any heavy discussion with this man. Things are still so new, and we are doing so well. I don't want to screw things up.

Obviously, I forgot to turn the subtitles off my face, because Dustin can see my concern loud and clear.

"You okay?" he asks, squeezing my hand. "You aren't already regretting coming with me, are you?"

I shake my head. "No."

"Did you leave your hair straightener on?" he guesses.

I scoff. "I hope not. It's in the backseat."

"Everything okay, then?" His voice is softer. He sounds genuinely concerned.

I shift in my seat. I guess it's now or never, at least for this part. "Dustin, do you want to have another kid?"

He pauses for a second. "Like... are you offering or...? I mean, I guess you aren't going to tell me you're pregnant with my baby since we haven't..." he trails off.

I roll my eyes and shake my head. Leave it to him to joke about the conversation that I was stressing over.

"No. I'm not knocked up, nor am I trying to be. It's quite the opposite, actually." I admit. "I'm not looking to have kids. I just wanted to know what you want before we get too far."

He deadpans. "Well, okay. I mean, Corbin is probably going to take it pretty hard that we are going to get rid of him, but he's almost eighteen. He will be okay."

I let out a groan and lightly smack his arm. "You know what I mean. Obviously, Corbin will be a part of your life forever, and I adore that kid. I don't want to have any babies on my own."

Dustin nods, looking out over the steering wheel before pulling over to the side of the road, on the edge of town. He picks up both of my hands this time. "That is totally fine with me. If you don't want babies, I support you. If you want babies, I support you. If you want fifteen cats, I'll support you."

I let out a small laugh and look down at my lap. "Better be careful. I am not above pushing the boundaries with a dozen or so cats."

He squeezes my hand. "Honestly, this is a relief. I mean, if you wanted to have a kid or two, I'd be open to it. I think every person who wants to have a kid of their own should have the opportunity. But I'm not going to push you to do it. Corbin is almost an adult, and the thought of starting over is slightly terrifying."

"Good," I say just above a whisper. "I have really been worried that I'm not going to be able to give you the life you want. I want to make you happy."

He leans forward and gently kisses my lips. "This. Right here with you is exactly the life I want. Just being who you are has answered every prayer of mine. You make me so happy... much happier than I've been in a very long time."

"Me too," I admit, meaning it more than he could ever know.

Then, I settle in next to him, resting my head on his shoulder as we make the drive towards Arkansas.

* * *

It's just after 4:00 when we arrive at the cabin.

The drive in was beautiful, which isn't a surprise because Arkansas is one of the most gorgeous states I've ever seen. It really doesn't matter how many times I've traveled here; I always seem to be in awe of the hills and winding roads.

"Alright, this is it," Dustin says, putting the truck in park. "Home sweet home for the next four days."

I open my door and step into the gravel drive, taking a moment to really get a good look at the cabin. Dustin had, of course, shown me pictures before we arrived, but they did it no justice.

This is exactly what I would expect when someone mentions a cabin. The structure itself was built from wood logs, with a green metal roof. The front of the porch runs the entire width of the house, with two wooden rocking chairs on one side and an oversized wooden porch swing on the other.

Dustin catches me eyeing the swing. "I knew you'd love that thing. That was the deciding factor between this cabin and another one down the road. I could already picture you lying there curled up with a book."

I stand on tiptoe and kiss his lips gently. "You know me too well."

Without another pause, I walk towards the porch and climb onto the swing. The cushion is springy and is the size of a twin mattress. It's large enough for the two of us. I lie down and scoot over, making sure to leave room for him to join me.

"What do you think the owners would say if we just took this home with us?" I ask, as I stretch out, cozying into the throw pillows.

Dustin snorts. "How about you just let me build you one of your own? I'm not really interested in being banned from coming back here one day."

I roll my eyes dramatically. "Fine. Mr. No sense of adventure. But, you're going to have to build me a back porch to hang it from, too. How are you at construction?"

He smirks as he lies down next to me. He props his head up on one hand and looks down at me. "I'm no professional, but I know a few things about carpentry. I bet for the right price I could fix you up."

"Oh, really? And what kind of payment are you expecting?"

I ask, gently biting my lip. I run my hand over his chest and then gently stroke the side of his face, inviting him to lean in and kiss me.

Dustin blushes. "I could tell you, but what do you say we go inside and I show you instead?"

Chapter 24

"Is it hot?" I ask, shrugging off my cotton robe.

"You're hot in that bikini," Dustin looks me up and down as he takes a seat in the hot tub on the back deck of the cabin.

I look down at my new swimsuit. I panic-ordered it from Amazon in the middle of the night when I couldn't sleep the day after Dustin invited me to come on this trip.

Alex was at the house when it arrived, and I almost returned it after seeing how little it covers, but she convinced me to keep it. She said, if there is ever a place to wear a skimpy bikini, a hot tub with your new boyfriend is the place.

"And yes, the water is hot, too. But it feels good after the five-hour car ride. Get in, you'll get used to it really quickly."

Taking his advice, I step into the tub and sit down next to him. Once I'm settled, he reaches over to a nearby table and grabs two glasses of wine, handing one to me.

I take a sip of my wine before leaning my head back, resting it on the enclosure behind me. "Okay, I'm going to need one of these on my patio, too."

"I'll add it to my honey-do list," he teases.

"You're going to need another vacation by the time I'm through with you."

Dustin wraps an arm around my waist and pulls me in close.

"As long as you come too, I'm good with it."

My eyes search his for a beat. "You don't think you're going to get sick of me before this week is over?"

He shakes his head. "Nope. I'm more concerned about how I'm going to survive not being with you every night once we get back."

"Oh, I'm not that great."

Dustin takes a sip from his glass. "I doubt that very much."

"I snore," I admit to him. "At least I'm pretty sure I do. It's only when I'm really tired, but I could put a man to shame. And I have terrible morning breath."

"I would be concerned if you didn't have morning breath."

I let out a deep sigh. He's not going to make this easy.

"Sometimes, I'll go to the diner to pick up burgers and fries for Alex and me at work. Then, on the way back to the school, I'll steal a couple of fries from the bag and give her the container of fries I've been stealing from."

Dustin shrugs. "That's called the fry tax. You picked up the food, so it's actually illegal not to do that."

"I wasn't aware they had passed that law in Kansas."

"Oh yeah, it was on the news and everything."

Okay fine. Last confession. It's now or never. It's time to admit that I'm Maisie Bloomfield, the best-selling author of the sweetest and swooniest books that no one would ever suspect that I write. But, just as I'm about to open my mouth, Dustin's phone starts to ring.

He leans back and looks at the caller ID before letting out a loud groan. "Sorry, I have to take this. It's work."

I wave him off. "No problem."

Dustin climbs out of the tub and answers with a casual. "Hey, man, what's up?"

I settle into the water and look up at the starry night sky as I nurse my glass of wine.

I was so close to telling him. The words were right there on the tip of my tongue. Maybe tonight isn't the night after all.

A few minutes later, Dustin comes back. Placing his phone on the side table before climbing back into the water next to me.

I down the rest of my wine and lean over, placing the glass next to his. But I don't sit back down next to him. Instead, I turn and climb into his lap, straddling his body as I wrap my arms around the back of his neck.

He smirks and rests his hands on my hips. "Well, hello. I see you enjoyed your wine while I was gone."

"I did," I admit, leaning down and resting my forehead against his. "And I'm really glad you're back."

"Hmmm..." he hums in response. "So, am I."

* * *

"Okay, do we have everything we need?" I ask Dustin as he pays for parking in downtown Hot Springs.

"I think so," he shrugs. "I have my swimsuit on, and I can't imagine what else I'll need besides that."

I glance at my watch. "We're a little early, but the hotel where we are going has a bookstore downstairs and a coffee shop inside. Want to go wander around for a bit before we check in for our baths?"

"Lead the way."

So, I do as he says. However, no one could miss the Arlington Hotel, which is positioned right in the middle of downtown Hot Springs. This hotel, which is actually considered a resort, has over 500 guest rooms, in addition to a restaurant, a bar, a row of retail stores in the basement, and, of course, the bathhouse spa.

We enter the resort through the basement stairs leading down to the shops below. Our appointment for thermal baths and massages is not until 11:00, so we have about an hour to kill.

We spend some time browsing the bookstore, a record store, and an eclectic gift shop, before walking up a grand marble staircase and landing in the main lobby.

Once in the lobby, we buy a coffee from the coffee shop and take a seat near the bar, overlooking the stage, where a nearby sign advertises the band performing live tonight.

"This place is really neat," I tell Dustin as I gently shake my iced coffee to stir the flavors. "I think I'd like to stay here sometime."

"It's definitely haunted." Dustin laughs. "So, if we stay here, you should probably bring an Ouija board."

I shake my head violently. "Absolutely not."

"Really?" he raises a brow. "I thought you'd be into that sort of thing."

I chuckle. "Look, I love black cats and spooky stories as much as the next girl, but you will not catch me dead playing with a Ouija board. I tried that once, and I am still scarred for life."

Dustin leans in closer. "What happened?"

I shake my head. I can't believe I'm even talking about this. "I had an Ouija board when I was a teenager. I bought it from a yard sale, and my parents had no idea."

"Did it work?"

I shrug. "I don't know. I mean, my friends and I tried it at a sleepover, but we had no idea what we were doing. We were just stupid kids who were obsessed with that movie, *The Craft*. We thought the witches in the movie were so cool, and we wanted to be just like them."

I continue. "So, we got the board out, and we asked if anyone was there. I swear, the pointer moved all by itself, and it said yes, someone was there. Then, we asked how they died."

Dustin leans in even closer, sipping his iced coffee through the straw and never removing his eyes from me. "And what'd they say?"

I gulp loudly. "They spelled out the word murder."

Just the memory of it makes me shudder. "That was about the time I decided I did not want to mess around with that stuff anymore. My dreams of being a witch were over from there. That was too much for me."

"So, what happened to it?" Dustin asks as he glances across the lobby, watching a man walk through the revolving door.

"To what?"

"The Ouija board."

I let out a groan. "Well, we tried to burn it. But, it didn't work."

He laughs. "What do you mean it didn't work?"

"It just didn't work. We tried to burn it with a lighter, and that did nothing. Then, we dumped gas on it, thinking surely that would do the trick. The gas just burned off, but the board still didn't burn. It was the creepiest shit I've ever seen."

Dustin frowns. "That's... weird."

"Very," I agree. "And it was made out of the same stuff regular game boards are made of. That freaked me out, and I threw it away after that."

Dustin smirks. "You know what would have been funny?"

I deadpan. "What?"

"If your brother had found the board and taken it out of the trash, and put it under your pillow," he replies with a laugh. "That's the kind of thing I would do to my siblings."

I let out a groan and glance down at my watch. It's about time to check in for our appointment. "My brother would have absolutely done something like that... if he had known about it. Thank God he didn't, or I would still be in therapy."

* * *

"Okay, sweetheart, get completely undressed and wrap yourself in this."

The woman standing in front of me hands me a folded bed sheet and points to the dressing room behind me.

I take the sheet and examine it, turning it over in my hand. "Um, okay. But, I leave my swimsuit on, right?"

She frowns. "No, take it all off. Believe me, you're going to want it all off for this."

I bite my lip. "So, it's not a pool?"

"No. It's a bath," she replies with a raised brow.

I'm going to be honest. I'm not a fan of public nudity, but I'm an even smaller fan of confrontation. So, I take the sheet, strip down, and wrap myself in it before meeting Ms. Cynthia, the bathhouse attendant, back at the lockers.

I put away my things and then follow her, padding along on the cold tile floor as she leads me to a room full of cast-iron bathtubs.

"This one is yours," she says, as she dumps the lavender-scented bath salts I chose into the water. "Take off your sheet, and I'll help you climb in."

"But... I'm naked." I answer quietly. Suddenly, confrontation doesn't seem so bad after all.

She waves me off. "Honey, I've been doing this job for twenty-seven years; there's nothing I haven't seen. It's fine. Let's get you in the water."

Against my better judgment, I drop my sheet and climb into the tub, settling into the hot water.

Ms. Cynthia hands me a Styrofoam cup of ice water. "I'll be back in about an hour to get you," she says, pulling the curtain closed, causing the old metal hooks to slide along the curtain rod with a screech.

An hour? What the heck am I supposed to do for an hour? If I'd known I'd be lying here all naked and vulnerable, I would have at least asked to keep my phone or bring a book.

I wonder if I gave Ms. Cynthia fifty dollars, she'd run down to the bookstore and get me something to read.

I'd settle for reading the back of a shampoo bottle or cereal box at this point. Who in their right mind can lie in this water for an hour with nothing but their thoughts and a cup of ice water?

This should be illegal. I wish I had games on my watch. I'd kill for a good game of Snake right now. Honestly, I'd kill for anything to occupy my mind while I lie in this water.

After fifty-five minutes of being alone with my thoughts, I have the rest of my current novel planned out, my next novel outlined, and at least 30 different scenarios mapped out of how I could potentially die in this bathtub... and finally, Ms. Cynthia comes to rescue me.

She slides open the shower curtain and smiles much too brightly for someone who has to spend her days dealing with pruny bath bodies. "How are you feeling?"

"Bored," I admit. "But, relaxed."

"Good. Let's get you out of that water."

Ms. Cynthia offers me a hand and helps me remove my naked body from the now lukewarm water. Then, she gets to work wrapping me in yet another bedsheet. Once I'm safely swaddled and ready for what I can only assume is a toga party, she hands me yet another cup of ice water and leads me to the sauna.

"Go have a seat in there until you get hot."

I take the cup, nod, and step through the wooden door of the sauna. There are two other women inside, sitting on the bench, and they stop talking as I walk in to join them.

I smile awkwardly and then take a seat on the bench in the corner of the room.

"I don't know about you guys, but this is the weirdest cult I've ever joined," I say to the others, in an attempt to lighten the mood.

The mood does not lighten.

In fact, the two women turn to one another, roll their eyes, and leave me alone in the sauna.

Fine. I didn't want to be in a cult with you anyway.

I sit in silence for another four minutes —I time it— before I've finally had enough.

I down the rest of my water and step out of the sauna to find Ms. Cynthia waiting for me. She leads me across the tile floor and instructs me to take a seat in a plastic lounge chair.

I do as she says, lying back in the lounge chair, and then she proceeds to wrap my arms and legs in hot towels. Once I'm sufficiently swaddled, she adds a towel around my face.

"I'll be back in twenty minutes," she says.

"I'll be here," I reply.

For the next twenty minutes, I stare at the ceiling of the bathhouse, questioning all of the life decisions that have led me up to this point.

Finally, the twenty minutes have passed, and Ms. Cynthia returns.

"How do you feel?" she asks.

"Strangely wonderful," I admit.

And I mean it. My body doesn't ache. My skin is soft.

I thank Cynthia as she leads me back to the locker room. I use the bathroom and change clothes, and then check my phone. I have a text from Dustin.

Dustin: That was... quite the experience. I'll be down at the lobby bar whenever you get done.

I round the entryway to the lobby and find Dustin seated at the bar with a can of soda in front of him. As our eyes meet, his eyes widen, and he shakes his head.

"I thought you were never coming back. I've been down here for half an hour."

"Half an hour?" I scoff. "Did you not get the full treatment?"

He shrugs. "I sat in that bathtub for like ten minutes and played on my phone. Then I decided I was too hot, so I put on a robe and got out."

My jaw drops. "You had your phone? And a robe?"

"You didn't?"

Now I'm completely flabbergasted. "No! I had to lie in that tub for fifty minutes with nothing but my thoughts. Then, I didn't even get a robe. She wrapped me in a bed sheet."

Dustin snorts out a laugh. "You need a drink."

I shake my head. "I need several drinks."

He smirks. "I know just the place."

We exit the hotel through the revolving doors and make our way down the concrete steps towards the crosswalk. Within just a few minutes, we are stepping into the Superior Bathhouse

Brewery. We grab a seat inside and perch ourselves on a pair of barstools, allowing us to watch people roaming up and down the sidewalk.

A quick scan of the menu tells us that some of the beer brewed at the brewery is even made with water from the Hot Springs.

"This is magical healing beer," I inform him. "Which leads me to believe that my cheeseburger and fries will be healing as well."

Dustin nods. "Makes sense to me."

We place an order for a flight to share and lunch for each of us, then we settle into our seats to people-watch.

Dustin reaches over and squeezes my hand. "This was fun."

"I feel traumatized, yet refreshed."

"The beer will help," he reassures me just as our server returns with our flight.

"It sure can't hurt," I reply, picking up the first tiny glass to take a sip. The beer's taste hits my tongue, making it clear it could indeed hurt.

"Gross. What is that? Pickle juice?" I gasp.

Dustin laughs. "It's called Big Dill."

I pick up my water glass and take a large gulp. "Why would you order that?"

He shrugs and picks up the offending glass. "Curiosity, mostly." He takes a sip. "Hey, that might be really good as part of a Bloody Mary."

I crinkle my nose. "Ew."

Dustin cocks his head to the side. "Don't tell me you don't like Bloody Marys."

I shake my head. "No, and honestly, I'm not sure if I can trust anyone who likes to sit around drinking spicy ketchup water."

Dustin laughs. "Well, I guess that just means I have to prove myself, doesn't it?"

I pick up another small glass of beer, checking the menu to make sure this time it was one I ordered.

#14- The Beez Kneez- a honey, basil blonde ale

I take a sip, and the sweetest of the honey with the earthiness of the basil hits my tongue. "Now, that is more like it. I could sit around and drink this one."

Dustin offers me his. "Number four. Spicy Ride."

I look at the menu again. "It's made with Jalapenos?"

He nods, and against my better judgment, I try it.

Luckily, it does not set my mouth on fire. Instead, it's refreshing and a little green tasting. It's good. A little spicy but good. "Okay, yeah. I do like that one." I decide.

"So, have I redeemed myself?"

I roll my eyes. "I don't know. I'm still mad at you for getting a robe and your phone during your bath."

Dustin places a hand on my thigh and gently squeezes it. "Well, I'll see what I can do to make it up to you."

Chapter 25

After a couple more days at the cabin, Friday morning arrives much too quickly, and it's time to go home. Dustin and I are packing up the truck and getting ready to make the drive back to Kansas.

"You up for a little detour this morning?" he asks with an excited smile.

I raise a brow. "What kind of a detour?"

"You'll see."

After a stop at the gas station for drinks and breakfast sandwiches, Dustin uses his GPS to point us towards the Garvan Woodland Gardens.

I raise a brow. "We are detouring to go to the botanical gardens?"

He shakes his head. "No, we are detouring to see something near there. And don't you dare look it up, either. Just put your phone down and enjoy the drive."

I let out a laugh. "Fine."

I have to admit. I'm thankful for the command to stay off my phone. If I were staring at my screens, I'd have missed the sights: the winding roads and scenic overlooks that seem to allow you to see all the way across Arkansas.

After about a twenty-minute drive, we pull into a parking

spot for the botanical gardens.

Dustin opens his truck door and turns to face me. "You ready?"

"Are you going to tell me where we're going yet?"

"Nope. Come on."

And with that, Dustin steps out of the truck and walks around to my side. He opens the door and helps me climb down onto the pavement. Then he pulls out his phone to use the map again and leads me across the parking lot. I stop and read a sign.

"The Anthony Chapel? Dustin, are you taking me to get married?" I cross my arms in front of my chest. "Dang, you must have been so impressed by my cooking this weekend that you had to immediately wife me up."

"It wasn't your cooking skills that impressed me." He retorts, nudging me gently. "And no one is getting married today. So, don't worry, you're not going to have to take off running through the woods to escape me. I just wanted to see this place. I saw it on the map when I was looking around the area for things to do, and it looks neat."

With that, we follow the signs to a stone pathway, and it's not long before the most stunning chapel I've ever seen comes into view.

The structure of the chapel is made entirely of glass and wood, and it's situated in the middle of the forest, almost as though it were planted there. I have seen many beautiful things in my life, but this cathedral-style church is at the top of the list.

I pull the metal handle on the massive wood door, expecting it to be heavy and hard to move, but it's not. When we step inside the chapel, I am awestruck by the beautiful simplicity of the rows of wooden pews on either side of the aisle leading to a simple stage.

Dustin and take our time, taking in the scenery around the chapel. Just as we're leaving, Dustin pauses, picking up a brochure about wedding packages and shoving it in his pocket.

I laugh, but I don't stop him.

All these years, I've thought my dream was to hide a wedding from my family, but I guess if I were to have a wedding where people were invited, this wouldn't be the worst place to have it.

We are just pulling into Fawn Creek when Dustin gets a phone call. His phone is connected to the truck radio, so when the music stops, and the name Ava pops up on the screen, I am caught off guard for a second.

What woman wouldn't worry when her boyfriend is getting a phone call from a woman on a Friday afternoon?

However, Dustin doesn't hesitate to answer the call on speakerphone. "Hey, Ava. Are you calling me with some good news?"

"The best news," she confirms.

Instantly, I recognize her voice as the local real estate agent. In a town as small as Fawn Creek, everyone knows everyone. Especially, someone like Ava who helps just about everyone in town buy their houses.

Ava continues. "I have a listing that's hitting the market this weekend, and it's exactly what you are looking for: four bedrooms, two baths, five acres, with a shop and a storm shelter. They're asking $250,000."

Dustin and I exchange a glance. He shrugs. "When can I come see it?"

"How about 6:00, tonight?"

"We'll be there. Text me the address." Dustin replies quickly.

"You got it. See you tonight."

"See ya." He turns to me with a wide grin. "You are coming

tonight, right?"

"You want me to come?" I ask, obviously confused.

"Well, yeah, of course I do. I could use a second set of eyes on this place. Corbin and I are pretty desperate to get into our own place." He pauses for a beat. "And, like I said. I like having you around. Tonight's my last evening without Corbin before I go pick him up tomorrow. We could go see the house and then maybe grab a pizza and hang out?"

I smirk. "So, you're still not sick of me?"

Dustin picks up my hand and kisses the back of it softly. "I don't think I'll get sick of you anytime soon."

"I hope you're right." I laugh as he pulls into my driveway.

Alex's yellow Mini Cooper is parked next to mine.

Dustin laughs. "Who does that thing belong to?"

"Alex. She's probably feeding the cats." I pause for a second. "Or, she died days ago when she came over, and I'm about to go inside and discover her body."

Dustin snorts. "Well, that's not morbid or anything."

I roll my eyes. "I mean. I don't want it to happen. I'm just saying it's possible."

He shakes his head. "I'll be back to get you at 5:45, and we will go check this place out, okay?"

"I'll be ready."

We say our goodbyes, and then I grab my bag and push my way into the house.

Alex is sitting on the couch with Jinx stretched across her lap. She's petting his back, and he's soaking up every second of it, purring happily.

Spoiled cat.

"I was just about to leave when I saw his truck pull into the driveway. I didn't want to interrupt your makeout session."

Alex smirks.

I let my jaw drop dramatically. "We were not making out. We were talking."

"Oh, is that what we are calling it these days?" Alex teases.

"We were. He wants me to go look at a house with him tonight."

Alex's jaw drops. "A house? Gosh, you guys just slept together for the first time this week, and you're already moving in together? You must be really good at what you do."

I pick up a throw pillow and lightly smack her with it. "The house is for him, not for me."

"Well, it has to kinda be for you. He did ask you to come look at it."

"He just needs a second set of eyes."

"He wants your approval," Alex smirks. "He is buying this house for all three of you, whether you like it or not."

* * *

"Hey, guys!" Ava calls out as she climbs from her royal blue SUV and jogs towards us. Her long black hair falls over her shoulders, and she's wearing jeans with a blazer that is the same shade as her car. "This place is incredible, isn't it?"

"Yeah, I'm already sold, and I haven't even seen the inside yet." Dustin laughs. He turns and lets his gaze fall on the horizon. For miles, all you can see from here is the grass blowing in the breeze and the beginning of a cotton candy sunset.

"Well, crap, let's just sign the papers then." Ava jokes. "Easiest sale I've ever made."

I interject. "Maybe we should take a little peek inside while we're here."

Dustin sighs. "I guess we did come all this way. A whole two miles out of town."

"Follow me then," Ava beams. "As I said, this place isn't even officially on the market yet. We're waiting for the photographer to come by and get pictures, but I thought of you immediately when the seller reached out."

"Well, I'm glad you did," Dustin says, stepping through the oak front door into the entryway. "This is exactly the kind of place I had in mind. It's right outside of town, but still close enough that driving into Fawn Creek isn't a hassle."

"Absolutely," Ava agrees. "The house is in pretty good shape. It's not newly remodeled, but everything has been updated in the last ten years."

Dustin reaches for my hand and squeezes it while Ava goes on about the roof and the heating system. He nods towards a sign on the wall in the entryway that says *It's Good to be Home* in a black script font on a white background.

Oh, he is definitely making an offer on this place.

She leads us into the living room. "As you can see, this room is massive."

She's right. The living room is large, yet still cozy. It has dark hardwood flooring and beige walls. There's a large sectional sofa anchored in the middle of the room. One wall is lined with built-ins shelving, with a large television hanging in the middle.

"The built-ins are amazing, and there's plenty of room for lots of books and knick-knacks." She continues as she steps towards a closed door. "And the room over here is technically considered a bedroom, but I think it would be an excellent office."

She swings the door open, and we poke our heads inside.

One wall of the room is made up of three windows overlooking the field next to the house. The room itself is small, but it would be the perfect size for a full-size bed, or, like Ava suggested, a desk and some bookshelves.

"This could be your writing room," Dustin whispers to me.

My body freezes, and I turn to him with wide eyes. "What?"

His smile falls. "You said you wanted to write one day. This could be a good space to sit and write. It could be your office."

I swallow hard.

Right. I did say that.

Not that I ever told him that I'm already an author. Nor did I take into consideration that any room in this house is meant to be mine. At least not yet.

We follow Ava through the living room and dining room and into the kitchen.

I don't say it, but I think I love this place just as much as Dustin does.

Honestly, it's everything I could ever want in a house. The kitchen is huge with an island in the center and a granite countertop. The cabinets look new, and I can't help but think that what's in my kitchen wouldn't fill a quarter of them. There's so much space.

Dustin spends his time opening cabinets and running a hand along the granite. He is growing more and more in love by the second. Unless we walk into the garage and find a dead body lying on the concrete floor, he's going to make an offer.

Hell, even if there is a body, he still might go for it.

Dustin motions towards a door. "Is this the garage?"

"Yep!" Ava confirms. "Feel free to take a look out there. There's a large shop out back, too."

Dustin swings the door open wide, and I stand on tiptoe to

take a peek.

Just a normal two-car garage, with no dead bodies.

Thank goodness, too, because I had pretty much convinced myself there would be one out there.

From the kitchen, we walk past the laundry room, and then we are in the master suite.

The bedroom itself is massive. It's large enough to hold a king-size bed, and there's a built-in vanity with a chair along one wall.

The closet is the size of the bedroom I have now. The bathroom is quite large as well, of course, since it has to hold a soaking tub and a two-person shower.

"This is my favorite part," Ava informs us, motioning towards a door at the far end of the bathroom. She unlocks it and swings it open to expose a small wooden deck. On the deck are a hot tub and a small seating area. The deck even has outdoor curtains that can be closed for privacy. "The hot tub stays, and it works great," Ava says.

"Nice," Dustin whispers, squeezing my hand.

This causes memories of our hot tub in Arkansas to rush back, and I know I'm blushing because my face is so warm.

Dustin steps further onto the deck, examining the ceiling. "I could build one of those porch swings right here," he informs me with a smile. "One like we had at the cabin."

I swallow hard, imagining the two of us wrapped in a blanket, overlooking the horizon, with a glass of wine in hand. This really could be a place for us.

After making a trip to the other side of the house, to tour the two guest bedrooms and the other bathroom, as well as a half bath off the kitchen. We make our way outside to check out the shop.

"Okay, I'm sold," Dustin grins, as we finish the tour. "Where do I sign? Can I move in tomorrow?"

Ava laughs. "Well, what we will do is I'll go home and write up an offer, and we will get it sent over to them. They are pretty motivated, so I bet you'll hear something by tomorrow afternoon."

Dustin rubs his hands together excitedly. "Well, let's get it done then. I'm ready."

Chapter 26

"Well, Corbin, how was Texas? I haven't had much of a chance to chat with you since you got home."

I'm standing at my kitchen counter, chopping vegetables to add to the large plastic salad bowl in front of me. I have fries in the oven, and Dustin is in the backyard, cooking burgers on the grill.

It's the weekend after our trip to Arkansas, and the boys are over at my house for dinner for the first time. Dustin and I decided that, since they will be moving into their new house in the next six weeks, we might as well get used to hanging out together more often.

Corbin is seated across from me on a barstool, sipping on a can of Dr. Pepper.

"It was awesome," he says, setting his can down on the counter with a clink. "One night we stayed up playing Roblox until 4 in the morning. His mom didn't even care."

I let out a laugh. "Well, that does sound awesome. I'm glad you had fun. And I'm glad you got to go. I know it's been hard moving away from your friends."

Corbin shrugs. "It's gotten easier here. I can't wait to move into the new house so Garrett can stay with me this summer. Dad said we will make sure the guest room is ready so he can have his own room while he's here. And he can stay for a week."

I toss the rest of the cucumber into the bowl. "That'll be perfect. I knew that house wouldn't be too big after all. You boys will have that house all filled up in no time."

Corbin looks down at his soda. "Ms. Calhoun?"

"You can call me Kristen. Unless we're at school."

He smiles. "Okay, Kristen? Are you going to move in with us?"

This question rattles me enough that I have to stop what I'm doing. "Did your dad say I was?"

Corbin shakes his head. "No, but you guys are really dating now, and we're hanging out over at your house on a random Saturday..."

I let out a soft chuckle. "Listen, your dad and I just started this whole dating thing. Navigating a new relationship is a lot of work, so don't worry, we are not going to rush into anything."

Corbin nods. "Okay. Well, so that you know. I don't totally hate you being around." A smile tugs at the corner of his mouth as he makes this admission.

"Well, thank you. I don't totally hate being around you guys either."

Before the conversation can go any further, Dustin walks through the side door of the house into the kitchen. He slides a plate of grilled hamburger patties onto the counter and pauses to look at us. "You guys hungry?" he asks.

"Starving," I reply.

"Let's make our plates and eat outside." He suggests. "It's a beautiful evening, and we all know that Spring in Kansas only lasts for a week. Might as well take full advantage of it while we can."

So, Dustin, Corbin, and I make our plates and carry them out to the backyard, taking seats around my wooden picnic table —a table that has not gotten nearly enough use over the years. Hopefully, that will change now that Dustin and Corbin are in my life. I have a feeling a lot of things are going to be changing.

"I'll be back. I'm going to run to the bathroom," Corbin says, standing from his seat. He walks into the house, and Dustin reaches across the table to squeeze my hand.

"Thanks for having us over tonight."

"Thanks for cooking for me," I reply with a shrug. "Feel free to come over anytime, as long as you are going to feed me."

"Got it." He smirks. "Well, before too long, I'll be cooking for you in my fancy new kitchen, too."

"That kitchen is incredible. I'm going to be honest, I see a lot of great meals in my future."

His voice softens and lifts a hand to touch my cheek gently. "I see a whole lot of you in my future. And I hope I'm right. I love you so much."

The words leave his lips, and for a second, they take my breath away. This is the first time he's told me he loves me, but somehow it comes so effortlessly that it seems he says it all the time.

"I love you, too," I whisper back.

Dustin and I pause in the moment, holding hands across the table while this admission hangs in the air between us. We're so lost in the moment, we almost don't notice the sound of Corbin's voice.

"Uh, what's this?" Corbin interrupts. He crosses the yard towards us, and he has a stack of papers in his hand.

Immediately, I know what he's holding. It's Maisie's newest manuscript. I finished writing it last night and printed everything out so I can read it over this weekend. And now it's in the hands of my boyfriend's teenage son.

"Um... well..." I begin, but Corbin hands the stack directly to Dustin. "There's a note on top that says 'check Dustin's eye color'. I just thought you should see this."

Dustin furrows his brow and takes the papers, reading the title page. "Who is Maisie Bloomfield and what does she want with my eye color?" he asks, flipping through the stack.

I swallow hard. "I can explain."

Dustin looks up at Corbin. "Hey, Corbin. Why don't you go inside for a second? Kristen and I need to talk."

Corbin pauses for a beat. "Am I in trouble?" he asks quietly.

"No," Dustin replies quickly. "We just need a minute, okay?"

Corbin nods and spins on his heel, walking towards the house.

Once he's inside, I brace myself for Dustin to speak, but he doesn't. His eyes continue to scan the pages in front of him as he inspects the contents of my manuscript while I pace in the grass in front of him.

Finally, he speaks up. "Kristen, what am I even looking at right now. I'm so confused."

I swallow hard. I knew I was going to have to come clean, but this is not the day I intended to do it.

"I am Maisie Bloomfield. I write romance novels under a pen name. No one knows. You're the first person I've ever told."

Dustin raises a brow. "How long has this been going on? This Maisie thing?"

I grimace slightly. "Five years."

Dustin doesn't respond; instead, he continues flipping through the pages and reading. "Wait. Is this Darren guy based on me? Is that why you needed my eye color? Is this book about us?"

I shake my head quickly. "No, it's not about us. You just inspired the character I created."

He pauses to read a little more and then looks up at me with a hurt expression on his face. "You wrote about the hot tub at the lake?" He raises his eyes to meet mine. "I thought that was just... ours. I didn't know it could end up in a book."

"It was real for me too." I pause for a beat. "I wasn't trying to turn it into something less than what it was."

Dustin shakes his head and glances towards the house. "That's not what this feels like. Listen, I need to go. I need to think things over. I'll call you later."

Before I can respond, Dustin makes his way across the yard and through the back door of the house, leaving me standing alone in my yard, surrounded by discarded plates of our half-eaten dinner. And I wonder where I'll go from here.

* * *

My mom slides a cup of coffee across the worn linoleum table towards me. I'm sitting in my parents' tiny apartment over their diner with a tear-soaked face and a broken heart.

The second Dustin left, I cleaned up the mess from dinner and ran to the one place I knew I could always turn to—my parents' house.

While my parents haven't always lived in the apartment over the diner—they sold the house after I moved out on my own—the kitchen table has remained the same.

Growing up, whenever I had a problem to solve, whether it be math homework or friendship advice or a decision on where to go to college, I always knew I could sit at this table, and my mom would help me figure it out. And she's never let me down.

Over my lifetime, so many things have changed, but this table covered in speckled yellow linoleum never has. The familiarity has always been such a comfort to me.

Even while I feel like I'm coming undone.

"I still don't understand," Mom shakes her head. "You are Maisie Bloomfield."

I nod. "Yes, that's my pen name."

"And why have you been keeping this a secret all this time?" She sips her coffee. "It doesn't make sense why you wouldn't have just written under your own name to begin with. Or at the very least, told someone what you were doing."

I shake my head, looking down into my mug. "I don't know. When I started, I never imagined it would get this far. I just wanted to see if I could write a book. I didn't mean to become a best seller. I wasn't even sure anyone would think it was good."

Mom smiles softly. "Well, you did it. In fact, you wrote a whole bunch of really good books. I would know. I've read them all. Twice."

I let out a soft chuckle. "Thank you."

Mom continues. "That's no small feat and nothing you should be ashamed of."

"I didn't think anyone would care," I admit with a shrug.

Mom squeezes my hand. "Of course we care. I am so proud of what you've accomplished. You need to show the world who you really are."

I nod, sitting in the silence of their apartment for a beat.

Mom smirks. "For what it's worth. I've always known this part of you existed."

I roll my eyes. "Oh really?"

She laughs. "Yes, of course, even when you were a kid, you were drawn to the softer, sweeter things in life. Fairy tales and happily ever afters... and you always did what you could to bring joy to everyone around you. Under that tough exterior, you've always been a lover, and I think it's time you let the rest of the world see that part of you, too. This might be the moment that pushes you towards that. It's long overdue."

I chew on my bottom lip. "I guess there's no time like the present. I probably should make it known to the world before someone else does. Not that I think Dustin and Corbin would ever do that, but maybe you're right. Maybe this is my opportunity to show everyone who I truly am."

She nods. "I believe your secret is safe with them, but there's no reason to keep quiet. You should be shouting it from the rooftops. This is something to be proud of."

"You're right. Better late than never, I suppose."

* * *

By the time I finish the drive back across town to my house, my body feels as though it's bubbling over with anxiety.

I walk inside, take a seat in my office, and use a candle to prop up my phone. And then, without hesitation or even a plan in place, I hit record on my first TikTok video.

"Hi, friends. It's me. Maisie Bloomfield." I swallow hard as soon as the admission hangs in the air in front of me.

"Except, Maisie isn't my real name. My real name is Kristen, and I'm a high school English teacher in Southeast Kansas who happens to be a hopeless romantic and a sucker for a happily ever after."

"When I started writing as Maisie five years ago, I had no

230

idea that my books would go viral one day. I just loved reading small-town romances, and I wanted to try writing one myself. So, I did."

I let out a soft chuckle. "And then I wrote another and another...and so on. I never meant to hide my identity. I never tried to be secretive. I wrote using a pen name because, honestly, I figured it would be easier if I failed. If my books sucked, then no one would know any better."

"But that didn't happen. Then, by the time my books started to take off, I couldn't find an easy way to step out of it."

I pause for a second, taking a deep breath, for what feels like the first time in ages.

"I know this might be surprising, especially for people who know me in real life, but it's time to stop hiding this part of me." I smile softly into the camera. "So, here I am. I'm done hiding. I'm going to make social media pages for Maisie and start sharing book updates and publishing news, and I will, of course, post here, too. I hope you'll follow along."

I hit the post button and stand from my desk, but I don't move.

I'm not sure what I expect to happen. Maybe that my laptop will explode, or a crowd of angry people will appear on my doorstep, or perhaps I'll wake up and find out that this has all been one very long dream.

But none of those things occur. Instead, I stand in the silence.

Until my phone rings.

It's Alex.

I hit the speakerphone button and take a seat at my desk. I have a feeling it's going to be a while before I can be productive. "Hi."

"Kristen Marie Calhoun!" Alex squalls into the phone. "Are

you kidding me right now?"

"Who is this?" I tease, trying to keep my voice steady.

Alex isn't buying it. "You are Maisie Bloomfield? Are you kidding? You wrote all of those books that made me laugh, cry, and swoon, and you didn't say a word?"

She doesn't pause long enough for me to answer.

"You wrote some of the most romantic and touching dialogue I've ever heard in my life? And you sat in that chair at book club, and let us gush over you, and you said nothing?"

"Ta-da," I reply, keeping my voice steady.

"I am flabbergasted," Alex says with a groan. "I thought I was your best friend, and you've been hiding this from me for all this time? And I had to find out on TikTok, of all places?"

"In my defense, we've only been friends for like 8 months." I tell her, "and by the time we met, I was already used to hiding this from everyone I knew."

Alex groans. "I wish you had told me."

I nod. "I know. I should have. I wanted to, and truly, I planned to. But, it just kept getting more complicated... and maybe I chickened out a bit."

"What did Dustin say?" Alex asks. "You did tell him, right?"

"Oh, he knows." I groan. "But, he didn't find out from me, and he's having a little trouble processing."

Alex pauses, "I don't get it. Is he mad?"

"Let's just say that he got a peek at my newest story, and he heavily inspires the male lead. He feels a little taken advantage of."

"Oh."

I swallow hard. "I just have to figure out how to handle this without losing myself in the process."

Chapter 27

By the time I'm crawling into bed on Saturday night, I've made some progress.

I have a substitute teacher scheduled for Monday.

As much as I hate missing work, and I hate writing up sub lesson plans even more, I need another day at home to get everything sorted out.

Besides, I'm not quite ready to go to school and face Corbin. As much as Dustin is mad at me, I have to admit, I'm not super happy with Corbin either. He shouldn't have been in my office. He shouldn't have been nosing around at my desk or reading my papers. I feel like he invaded my privacy, and that's a level of violation I will have to work through on my own.

The rest of my long weekend is spent deep in the trenches of editing. Of course, this was already my plan for the weekend, but I have to admit I wasn't planning on going over it with a fine-tooth comb, removing anything that seems a little too much like Dustin.

By the time Monday afternoon rolls around, I'm satisfied with my draft, and I hope he will be, too. I've removed the hot tub scene. And I've paid special attention to the main male character, Darren.

In fact, his name isn't even Darren anymore. It's Chris.

Chris is still the charming, blue-collar lead that he was when I wrote him. He's still rough around the edges, with calloused hands and a kind heart, but he no longer resembles the man I'm in love with. Instead, I've focused more on the love story that brews between the characters and less on feeling as though I'm writing fan fiction about my boyfriend.

Dustin generally gets home around 5:30, so at 4:00 on the dot, I finally walk out of my pretty pink writing lair and start to get ready.

After a long shower and a thorough wash of my hair, I spent a lot of time on my novel and not nearly enough time on my greasy hair over the last couple of days—I get myself ready to face Dustin. I fix my hair and makeup, then put on a new outfit—a hot pink blouse with a pair of dark-wash boot cut jeans. I suppose if I'm going to be a rom-com author, it's time to start dressing like one.

Then, at 5:15, I grab my newly printed manuscript and climb into my car. With shaky, sweaty hands, I drive to Dustin's parents' house and park at the curb, waiting for him.

Like clockwork, Dustin arrives home at 5:30. I watch as he steps out of his work truck, his dirty boots hitting the pavement, but I still don't move from my car. For a second, I consider leaving.

I sit, frozen, as he gathers his lunchbox and his coffee thermos from the backseat, and I nearly chicken out. But that's when our eyes meet.

He attempts to smile, but the smile doesn't reach his eyes. It's forced. He's still mad at me, and for a second, I wonder if there is any chance of fixing this at all.

But it's too late. I can't leave. He knows I'm here.

The only way to move through this is to face it head-on.

I climb out of the car, grabbing the pile of paper from my passenger seat before crossing the street towards him. "Hi," I say, carefully.

"Hi." His tone is gruff and hollow, and it makes my heartache even more, knowing that this same man told me he loved me just days ago. How did it all fall apart so quickly?

I swallow hard, fighting back tears. "Dustin, I'm sorry you were hurt. I never intended for you to find out this way, or for it to feel like I was exposing something between us."

He shakes his head. "I'm not mad that you hid it, Kristen. I'm mad because I felt like our private relationship was suddenly on display for the whole world to read. It felt like an invasion of my privacy."

I chew on my bottom lip. "Kinda like Corbin taking it from my office and giving it to you was an invasion of mine."

Dustin leans against his truck with a deep sigh. "Yeah, and he's not going unpunished for that one, either. He's grounded and has listened to a long lecture about not going into places that don't belong to him. I'm sorry. That's not the way he was raised, and he's absolutely not going to pull something like that again."

I feel a twinge of guilt knowing that Corbin is in trouble, but I'm glad Dustin addressed it, too.

"That was my first draft. It wasn't intended to be seen by anyone but me," I explain. "But, reading it back, I understand why you were upset. I'm sorry for making you feel like you're just a character in a story. That wasn't how I ever saw you. To me, this has always been real. In fact, this is the first time in my adult life that I have really experienced the kind of love stories I write about. You made me happy, and that sparked a creative fire in me that I've never felt before. Hurting you was not my intention."

Dustin steps towards me and picks up my hand that's not gripping the manuscript. Then, he pulls me gently towards him. "Kristen—"

I interrupt him and hand him the stack of papers. "I made some changes. I removed the parts I thought crossed a line. I want you to read it knowing I took that seriously."

Dustin takes the pages, looking down at the top page. It's the dedication page. He pauses to read it.

This book is dedicated to the one who taught me that happily ever after can exist in real life, after all. I love you.

He looks up at me with a soft smile. "Thank you. You didn't have to change your whole book. I probably overreacted, but it was a lot in the heat of the moment. I panicked because I didn't want to think about the fact that my kid or the kids at school would be reading about our private life. It really freaked me out. You're an incredible writer, and I don't want to mess that up by telling you what you can and can't put in your books. I crossed the line."

I shake my head. "Listen, the freak out was valid. Maybe if I had told you myself instead of the way you found out, it would have been easier to digest."

"Maybe," he agrees. His tone has changed since I arrived. It's softer, more gentle.

I clear my throat. "I need you to understand something. You were never just a character. I love you, for real. I've written fifteen books, and I thought I understood love. But then I met you—and I actually felt it. I don't want to throw that away."

Dustin takes one more step towards me and places a hand

along my jaw, steadying my face as he leans in to me. "Kristen, I love you so damn much. I'm going to do everything I can to help you feel this, for as long as I'm alive."

"Even if you have to live with me as Maisie Bloomfield, romance author?"

Dustin nods. "I love you. Every piece of you and I want to make sure you never feel like you have to hide those parts ever again."

Chapter 28

Tuesday morning, I walk through the doors of Fawn Creek High, cautiously but with my head held high.

My secret is out. My books are nothing to be ashamed of, other than the fact that they prove I'm more of a softy than I've led people to believe.

Even if I had kept that hot tub scene, my stories are fade-to-black, so nothing explicit would have happened on page. There's no reason to be worried about being pulled in front of the school board after my TikTok post yesterday.

So why am I still so damn nervous about going back to work?

"Good morning," I greet Sharon carefully as I step through the door to the office and check my mailbox for anything I might have missed while I was gone.

She looks up and smiles gently. "Feeling better, sweetie? We missed you around here yesterday."

I nod. "Yes, thank you. I feel much better."

And it's not a lie. I do feel a lot better. After mending things with Dustin last night, I went home lighter and more confident than I've felt in a long time.

"So," Sharon adds, drumming her nails on her desk, "from what I understand, I'm in the presence of a best-selling author."

Sharon's words cause me to freeze in place. Word certainly doesn't take long to get around in Fawn Creek.

She continues. "Very sneaky of you, Ms. Calhoun. But it is also very exciting. I've been a Maisie Bloomfield fan for a while, you know. I'll have to bring in all my books to have you sign them."

I let out a soft chuckle. "I'd be happy to. But, for now, I'd better get to my room so I can be ready for the kids."

Sharon gives me an understanding nod, but keeps going. "I hope being a big-time author isn't going to make you want to leave us."

I shake my head. "No, of course not. Don't worry. Teaching is my first love, and I have no plans to go anywhere. I'd miss the kids too much."

A look of relief spreads across her face. "Good. The kids would miss you, too. And so would the rest of us. You'd be a tough act to follow, that's for sure."

"I'm not going anywhere, I promise," I say, stepping out of the office and into the main hall.

I have to admit, it feels good to be appreciated.

Once inside my classroom, I turn on the lamps, get my coffee pot ready for the day, and then take a seat at my desk to review the substitute teacher's notes.

Ms. Calhoun,

I hope you're feeling better. Your classes were well-behaved and stayed on task for the most part. Although I will say there was a lot of whispering about their teacher being a famous author. Congratulations!

Ms. Miller

Well, that settles that. The kids are talking.

Today could be a lot. It could be exciting, or it could be impossible to keep the kids on track. Either way, I have to get through it.

The first two hours of the day go by pretty smoothly, with a minimal amount of interruptions. However, Corbin is in my third hour class, and I've been bracing myself all morning to see him.

He wastes no time coming to class long before the bell rings. It's almost as though he was standing in the hall waiting for the class change.

Corbin places his books on his desk and walks directly towards mine. He pauses in front of me, nervously swaying as he shifts his weight from one foot to another.

"Hi," I say, keeping my voice as steady as possible. "What's up?"

Corbin begins to speak, keeping his voice low. "I'm really sorry about taking those papers from your office and showing them to my dad. I know I shouldn't have been in there. I was looking for the bathroom, and I saw that post-it note on top of the pile of papers, so I was being nosy."

I nod in response. "Thank you for the apology."

Corbin lets out a deep breath, relaxing a bit. "You're the first girlfriend he's had since my mom died. This is the first time he's really seemed happy in a long time."

He pauses to look over his shoulder to make sure no one is standing behind him. "He was really sad, and he was in bed a lot. He wasn't my dad anymore. But now that he's met you, he's back."

I feel the sting behind my eyes, and it takes everything in me not to get up and hug this kid. But I stay where I am. This isn't a moment I want to make messy for him—or for me.

"Now, he's back to telling me stupid dad jokes and singing in the shower and whistling for no reason. He's happy again. So, when I saw your book with someone else's name as the author and the note, I just panicked because you were hiding the truth from him. So, I showed him."

This causes a tear to roll down my cheek, but I quickly wipe it away.

"Corbin, I get why you did what you did. But my work, my writing, my life—it's not something to investigate again. Okay?"

He nods.

"Good. Because I like you, I like your dad. But I need respect to go both ways."

Corbin nods. "Deal. And just so you know, I learned my lesson." He shoves his hand in his pocket and pulls out a flip phone. "I'm so grounded that my dad took my smartphone, and I have to carry this thing around for the next month." He sighs and slides it back in his pocket. "Believe me, he made sure I learned my lesson."

The bell rings, signaling the beginning of class, and I stand from my seat to address the kids.

"Alright, boys and girls. I hope you had a good day yesterday, but now it's time to get back to work. Here's your journal assignment for today... *If I wrote a book, it would be about...*"

* * *

The rest of my day goes by without issue. A few girls bring in books for me to sign, and I oblige. I might as well get some practice at signing my pen name.

Tyler has already emailed asking me to do a signing at the store. I figure after lying to the girls about who I am, I owe it to her to let her host my first official book signing.

During my lunch break, I walk into the teachers' lounge to heat my leftovers in one of the shared microwaves. I hit the start button and then take a seat at a table, pulling my phone from my back pocket to do some scrolling while I wait.

The social media accounts I set up after my introduction post have exploded. Across all three platforms, I have nearly fifty thousand followers and more notifications than I could ever wade through.

I'm not even going to try. Instead, I close the app and place my phone face down on the table. It's strange how quickly your private life can become public noise. But it still feels like mine. That part doesn't scare me as much as I expected.

My microwave dings, telling me that my leftover chicken and rice casserole is ready. So, I grab the container and return to my seat, looking forward to eating in silence.

Generally, I take my lunch back to my room to work while I eat, but today is different. I know I'm highly unlikely to get a moment of peace in my classroom with the news about Maisie freshly circulating. Today, I need to hide from the kids more than I need to hide from the teachers. The silence doesn't last long, but at least the interruption isn't a bad one.

"Hey," Hannah calls out casually as she walks into the room.

She's wearing a long-sleeve floral dress, and her long, dirty blonde hair falls in loose waves over her shoulders. "How are ya?"

"I'm good," I brace myself for her to say something about the whole Maisie situation, but she doesn't.

Instead, she pulls her floral-covered lunch bag from the

fridge and points to an empty chair across from me. "Can I join you?" she asks.

I nod. "Of course, be my guest."

Hannah takes a seat and assembles the salad she brought for lunch today. "How are things?" she asks before taking her first bite.

"Good. A little crazy, but good." I smile.

She furrows her brow. "Crazy how?"

Okay, either she's messing with me, or she lives under a rock.

I place my fork down and eye her suspiciously. "You didn't see the video on your social media?"

She throws her head back and laughs. "No. I might be the only living adult on this planet that doesn't do social media."

I pause, taking in what she just said. "Really? That's impressive. Well, do I have a story for you."

Hannah eats her salad and listens with wide eyes as I tell her my story: my pen name, my rise to fame, and my admission to the world.

By the time I've laid it out on the table, there's nothing between us but a couple of half-empty food containers.

"That's... insanely cool," she says, shaking her head. I'm going to have to pick up one of your books. I love a good rom-com."

They are a good distraction from all the heaviness of the world," I agree. "Sometimes you just want something sweet and happy and a little predictable. Nothing beats a good happily ever after."

"Especially when your life feels like a complete dumpster fire," Hannah agrees, poking around at her remaining salad with a fork.

She looks sad. I've never seen her look anything but happy,

and it honestly breaks my heart.

I raise a brow. "Are things okay? Is it the job? The kids? If the kids are giving you crap, I will fight them for you. Well, maybe not fight them, but I'll give them some really annoying assignments."

Hannah shakes her head. "No, the job and the kids are great. It's just life stuff, but I'm going to be okay. I have to make it til summer."

"I think we are all ready for a break," I admit.

"Now that, I won't disagree with," Hannah smirks as she stands to pack up her lunch bag. "It was good talking to you, and I'll be sure to pick up a book. I could use some carefree summer reading. And who knows... maybe one day I can get you to write me a happily ever after of my own."

Chapter 29

6 weeks later.

"Oh my gosh, I am so freaking nervous," I say to Alex and Tyler. "I'm going to puke all over this stupid pink dress. What was I thinking agreeing to do a signing? There are so many people out there."

I'm pacing in the salon above Tyler's bookstore. I just had my hair and makeup professionally done, but it's still not enough to give me any confidence.

"I knew I should have covered the windows before you got here," Tyler smirks. "You're going to be fine. All of these people are here to see you. They pre-ordered like a zillion books, and they are here to have you sign them. Because you are an incredible author."

I deadpan. "No, I'm an incredible idiot. I like writing because I don't have to talk to people. It's solitary. I can type the words and change them a million times if I need to before putting them out there for other people. I can't be trusted to speak." I shake my head violently. "What if I say something stupid? What if I get myself canceled five seconds after everyone on the planet finds out who I am? This was a terrible idea."

Alex places a hand on my shoulder. "Hey, so you're spiraling right now, and you need just not to do that."

I roll my eyes. I love Alex to death, but she is too optimistic. "Oh yeah, thanks. I'll flip a switch and stop."

She groans. "Listen, you can't back out now. The whole world knows who you are. So, here's what we are going to do. We are going to walk down the stairs, you are going to sit at your little table, and you're going to sign like two hundred books. And you're going to be fine because these people are so excited to meet you."

My phone vibrates from the pocket of my dress. I pull it out to look at it. "Dustin's here. Can he come up here?"

Alex shakes her head. "Nope, if you want to see him, you need to get down there. Your event starts in exactly 45 seconds."

I frown. "I kinda hate you."

"No, you don't. Now, are you going willingly, or am I going to have to drag you down the steps?"

I grumble. "Fine. I'll go. Just in case I start saying something stupid or completely unhinged, kick me."

"Oh, it would be my pleasure."

With that, I make my way down the creaky wooden stairs and find the interior of the bookstore filled to the brim.

Everywhere I look, I see smiling readers, clutching copies of my books. Some faces I recognize, but there are many more that I've never seen before.

I swallow hard and make my way towards the table Tyler set up for me. I take a seat in front of the hot pink-and-black balloon display and wait for Tyler to introduce me.

"Good morning, everyone!" Tyler shouts. "Thank you so much for joining us for Maisie Bloomfield's first-ever book signing. There's a lot you need to get through here today, so just please be patient while waiting in line. The book you pre-ordered is on the table. Just hand Maisie your paper with any personalization you are requesting, and she will sign your book."

With that, Tyler steps out of the way, ushering the first reader towards the table. I smile softly as a woman with long brunette hair slides her note card towards me.

"Just make it out to Mandy, please."

No matter how much I've practiced, signing my name in front of all these people suddenly feels like the most terrifying thing I've ever done. I scrawl my Maisie signature across the page and smile, sliding the book towards her. "Thank you so much for coming," I say.

"No, thank you for writing these stories," she replies. "I can't explain it, but these books have changed my life. Please don't ever stop writing."

I blink back tears and thank her once again, before Alex and Tyler work to get the line moving.

Now I understand why authors want to meet their readers. This is the motivation I need to keep going. Knowing that my stories touched even one person is enough to help me see that I'm doing exactly what I'm meant to do.

Over the next two hours, I sign so many books that my hand cramps and my face hurts from smiling, but I make it.

The last patrons say goodbye, clutching their books in hand as they make their way outside. Tyler closes the door behind them and locks it before turning towards me with a massive grin.

"Kristen, you sold more books today in this store than I have sold in the last month."

Alex chimes in, "Well, what can we say? Everyone in the world was dying to get their hands on the newest Maisie Bloomfield release. I have it on high authority that this is her best book yet."

I roll my eyes. "Who is that authority?"

"Me. Duh."

"You already finished? I just gave it to you yesterday." I shake my head.

"I stayed up all night reading," she confesses. "What can I say, I'm a super fan."

"You need a super life," I say with a smirk, so she knows I'm teasing.

"Okay, children. That's enough picking on each other." Dustin chimes in. "How about a late lunch? I'm starving."

"I could use a greasy burger right now," I admit. "But, do you think it's safe? I mean, I brought a lot of extra people to town today, do you think we will be able to eat lunch at the diner without it being some big spectacle?"

Dustin reaches out and squeezes my hand. "I think if you want people to continue to treat you like a normal person, you should just keep acting like one."

"Agreed," Alex chimes in. "And I'm not just saying that because I'm starving."

"Okay," I nod, and stand from my seat before glancing down at my dress.

At first, I considered changing. Normally, I wouldn't dare to wear something so bright and girly in public. Hot pink dresses and wedge heels are meant for Maisie, not for me. But, I think it's about time to let the Maisie part of me shine for the world to see.

Dustin interlaces his fingers in mine and pulls my hand to his mouth, gently kissing it. "You ready?"

I nod. "Yeah, let's go."

"I love you," he whispers. "And I'm so proud of you for

showing the world all of who you are."

"Thank you for loving all of me," I reply with a grin before standing on tiptoe to kiss his mouth.

The four of us walk out of the cozy bookstore and make our way down the sidewalk towards my parents' diner. While we wander along, I can't help but think of how much my life has changed in a matter of months.

I used to think of Maisie as a whole separate person—a hopeless romantic who loves flowers, poetic words, and the color pink.

But what I've come to realize is that all along, Maisie has always been me. I just wasn't ready to admit it. And now, we can finally live as one, for the whole world to see.

Epilogue

"I now pronounce you, man and wife. Dustin, you may kiss your bride."

Dustin wastes no time and turns to wrap an arm around my waist and pull me in close. His mouth finds mine, and for a second, I forget that we're standing on a stage in the glass Anthony Chapel in Arkansas while all of our friends and family watch us kiss so passionately in front of them.

We come up for air, and I let out a laugh as Dustin's face turns a bright shade of red. "I got a little carried away," he whispers.

"You think?" Corbin chimes in, but with a smirky grin to let us know we haven't embarrassed him too much yet.

The wedding officiant chimes in, "Ladies and gentlemen, I now introduce to you, for the very first time, Dustin and Kristen Crenshaw."

We turn towards the row of seats and pause for a beat as our small group of friends and family rise to their feet, clapping their hands in excitement.

I look back at Dustin and squeeze his hand. It may have taken me longer than I expected to get my happily ever after, but it was worth the wait. Every day feels like a fairy tale, and I can only imagine how many more stories this man will inspire me to write.

I've always believed every one of my heroines carried a piece of me.

But now, I can't wait to write story after story of men like him—and all the ways he loves me.

I have a feeling there will be more than enough to last a lifetime.

About the Author

Michelle Lynn Ross is the author of humorous and heart-warming small-town romances set in Kansas, in the fictional town of Fawn Creek. A Kansas girl at heart, she loves small towns, second chances, and characters who feel like friends. When she's not writing, she's reading, planning her next trip, hanging out with her husband and three daughters, or spending too much time on social media.

You can connect with me on:
- https://michellelynnross.com
- https://www.facebook.com/ThatsWhatShellSaid
- https://instagram.com/michellelynnrosswrites
- https://www.tiktok.com/@thatswhatshellsaid

Subscribe to my newsletter:
- https://michellelynnross.substack.com

Also by Michelle Lynn Ross

If you enjoyed *Checking You Out*, you might also love these stories set in Fawn Creek:

The Fawn Creek Series:
There's No Place Like Home
Small Town Famous
Single in a Small Town
Signed, Sealed, Delivered

The Fawn Creek Faculty Series:
Checking You Out

Standalone novella:
Back to You

9 798999 931061